ONE FOR THE ROAD

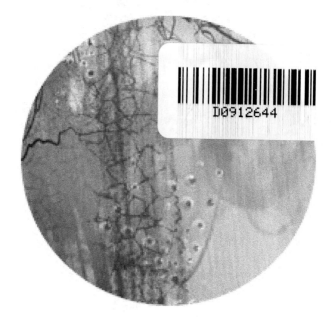

WESLEY
SOUTHARD

deadite
press

deadite press

DEADITE PRESS
P.O. BOX 10065
PORTLAND, OR 97296
www.DEADITEPRESS.com

AN ERASERHEAD PRESS COMPANY
www.ERASERHEADPRESS.com

ISBN: 978-1-62105-303-3

For Bob Ford.

May your hair be long and your liver stay strong.

For Miranda,

Heavy metal will never die ...

It's a shame we're not as lucky...

ACKNOWLEDGEMENTS

Many, many thanks as always to Kelli Owen and Bob Ford, Brian Keene and Mary SanGiovanni, Mike Lombardo for your massive amount of help and encouragement, Lex Quinn, Somer and Jessie Canon, the entire No*Con crew, Mark Duvall (RIP), Joseph Hunt and family, Mom, Dad, Sis, my lovely wife Katie, Nathan Brown for inspiring this story all those years ago (No more ham sandwiches, brother!), Matt Hayward and Jonathan Janz for their kind words, Mastodon because their music fucking rules, and to every band and musician that made me want to play. And most of all to Jeff Burk and Rose O'Keefe for their belief in my work. You all are the best.

"Heavy metal is immortal, but we're not."
—Rob Halford

"Dogs smoke in France."
—Ozzy Osbourne

I had always envisioned the highways of this great nation of ours as a woman—more precisely a road-hardened biker. You know the type: unbuckled on the back of a Harley, dyed blond hair as burnt as her golden skin, donned in leather, holding tight to the man-gorilla steering that battered hog. Sure, she looks like fun. But my God, how many of us have traveled across her, left our dusty trails and filthy skid marks behind? Thoroughfare for the young and old alike. From bikers to business men, sightseers to runaways, all have seen her at one point or another, and most have ridden her into the dying sunset, leaving something—a dream or a memory—not far behind.

But there's a darker side to her, a side most wouldn't dare cross. If you're not watching that scorched goddess, not giving her your full, undivided attention, she'll swallow you whole and shit you out like yesterday's bad Mexican dinner. Just another stain in the upper rim of life's filthy toilet bowl.

I wasn't watching. I wasn't heeding her advice, her consistent warnings to turn around, go home, don't look back...

This is what happened to us—the band—on that unforgivable day. Whether or not you choose to believe a word of this, well, that's your damn problem.

It happened.

March 10th

Let me start off by telling you I am not fucking crazy.

Even as I write this I can sense future readers of this memoir will be rolling their eyes by this point, wishing they'd never picked up this stupid notebook in the first place. Just a green spiral notebook, with mad scribblings by a mad man. Sure, I can see how you'd think that. Having a crayon drawing on the cover of a duck with a massive erection doesn't exactly scream "*Open me!*" But you're here, so...

What can I tell you about August twelfth? Good lord, our last free day before the rug was torn out from under us. For starters, let me inform you that, although I may not be crazy, I am indeed a dumb ass—and by dumb ass I mean I'm a musician. (Or was, I guess.) Let's break this down. When I was a young lad of thirteen, on the cusp of my awkward teenage years, I discovered music. No, not that hedonistic bullshit that MTV—or God forbid VH1—crams down our throats and expects us to happily digest, but real music. Music with style, an edge—one with a driving force that makes you think differently, dress in strange ways, speak words you didn't even think existed.

It was heavy goddamn metal!

In the short few months between seventh and eighth grade, a romance blossomed between me and the metal. Before that summer, the only CD's that kept me company were my father's. On the weekends, when dad had a few drinks—and *just* on the weekends, and *only* because he deserved them—he would take me aside, sit me down, and school me on what real rock and roll was all about. From Seger to Skynyrd, classic rock was not only his music, but now—with a wee bit of initial reluctance—mine. Big guitars and even

11

bigger hair, the rock gods of yore knew how to not only write the songs that made you sing but played the instruments that moved your soul. They commanded you to boogie, scream, and occasionally (if you're prone to utter idiocy) take someone's life in the name of all that was rock.

And I wanted to be one of them.

Guitar number one was an awful Stratocaster knock-off I received for Christmas, but damn it, I loved that stupid thing with all my heart. I quickly learned "Smoke on the Water" (every guitarist's first riff) and went on to teach myself Calling Dr. Love with ease. It came so easy, like my fingers were made to be placed across that fretboard, to form the power chords that set my young soul ablaze.

God damn it, I was finally a musician!

And thus, the beginning of my stupidity.

For a solid year, I took lessons and slowly gained the necessary knowledge and skill for the instrument. *This isn't a toy, boy*, Dad had reminded me on fairly regular basis. *You take the lessons and you learn the craft, so then one day you can make enough money to buy me a new house.* Sure, Dad, that's exactly why I started playing. Have another drink. You see, Mom wasn't around all that much because she was traveling around in space, searching for new planets and solar systems. Seriously, my mom's a true blue astronaut! It's a bit strange when I think about it now, but it's what Mom does. It's her life's work, her passion. I remember Dad reminiscing over those nights of musical lecturing that she had spent numerous years in the navy and the air force after they had met in college just to be accepted into NASA's space program. Dad was proud of her. So was I.

The problem now is I can't even remember what

she looks like. She was never around all that much. When she's not zipping around the galaxy, she's usually traveling across the country giving public appearances and speeches at colleges and whatnot. Dad's a school teacher, the absolute polar opposite of his wife. Sure, an odd couple, but they seemed to make it work... when she was around. But when she was away, well, Dad just got depressed.

Sorry, I don't want to get too far away from the point.

I won't bore you with the specifics of how or why hard music found me and held me lovingly in its arms, but I will tell you this: It hit me hard and fast, like a bullet right through the face. I suddenly knew my calling. I had a purpose. Within months my hair had grown to my shoulders, and my shirts progressively faded into the darker color spectrum. I wrote songs about death and destruction. Yes, I was the creepy kid in class who sat in the back of the room, waiting for 2:45 pm so I could go home and bash the shit out my beloved guitar.

I guess I'm digressing again. OK, back to August twelfth. Let's see if I can remember all of this.

***

"Goddamn, that's a smelly one!" Steve called out from the front of the van, his ass hanging out between the two front seats. He fanned his flatulence with a tattooed hand. Everyone laughed hysterically, covering their noses, pretending to be disgusted.

I wasn't laughing.

As usual, I had claimed my spot in the back row of the van. My home away from home. I didn't need to see the commotion. I heard it and instantly knew what they were carrying on about. By that point in time I couldn't even feign the slightest bit of interest in anything they did. Even the simple stuff like farts and belches—things that six months ago would have had me rolling with the rest of them—now made me cringe. Really, the last thing we needed was more gas. It was the middle of August, and the air conditioner was already broken. But you couldn't tell Steve that.

There were a lot of things I kept from Steve.

I had been lying in the back seat for the last several hours as the van trundled along, with my MP3 player strapped to my head. I found myself coming back to the same Johnny Cash greatest hits album I had been listening to for the last several weeks. I particularly liked "Delia's Gone" and "Get Rhythm", the simple melodies and shuffle rhythms, but since I had forgotten to charge the damn thing at our last stop, it died in mid-song. Irritated, I threw it into my backpack, along with my laptop and other electronic gadgets that kept me linked to the outside world. I knew I would have never been able to tell the other guys what I was listening to. I would have never heard the end of it. If it wasn't some blaring death metal album with the conventional *chug-chug-chug* guitar riffs—like they had droning from the van's speakers at that very moment—they wanted no part of it. That's why I never showed them my album lists. Kiss, Bob Seger, Heart, even Boz Scaggs.

Don't get me wrong. I love metal. I wouldn't have been traveling the continent, playing for a whopping three or four people a night, if I didn't. It was in my blood, but classic rock would always be my heart and soul.

So I kept my mouth shut.

I glanced up at the rest of the band who were gathered in the front two rows. They laughed and sang (or screamed) to the same Pantera album that had been spinning since the week before. Steve was somehow perched on the head rest of the front passenger seat, head banging to the thunderous beat, his long unwashed hair whipping through the air. Steve was our singer…if that's what you wanted to call him. Every night, he bawled abrasively into the microphone until he couldn't speak or stand—but the massive quantities of scotch before, during, and after the show didn't help much either. I never cared for the guy, nor would I ever. Just your regular, run-of-the-mill, smartass redneck. To Steve, most everything was a joke, and I tried to stay as far away from him as possible, especially on stage. I would be playing on my side, doing what I was born to do, and before I know it, I'm covered in Steve's spit and liquor, or my head would be gashed from a swinging microphone. "All in good fun," he'd say.

Look who's laughing now, Steve!

Vinnie sat behind Steve, his wooden sticks clacking away against the black rubber practice pad. It was his way of passing the time on our long stretches between towns. I had known Vinnie since high school, but I never talked to him much back then. At that time we were in rival bands and neither got along too well. But I had always found myself stunned by his amazing abilities as a drummer and respected the hell out of the guy, which was why I was ecstatic when he asked me to be part of this. He told me he had found out about this traveling band and wanted to see if I would audition with him, seeing as how both their drummer and guitarist had recently quit. A new city every night, playing the music we loved? Of course I was in.

Little did I know it was going to be a huge mistake. I could tell Vinnie wasn't all that happy either, but we were both stuck. His abilities—*our* abilities—were far beyond what Rot in Hell had to offer. That's why we both had a plan.

To his right sat Les, our know-it-all bassist. He tended to do what all bass players set out to do: be as fucking weird as possible. His jet black hair reached down to his knees, wild and unwashed. His dyed yellow beard, which if you looked at him dead-on it seemed to swallow his entire face, waved over his waistline and beer gut. Les was quite the opposite of me. He was a total snob. Like most musicians, he tended to be self-centered, even narcissistic, and no matter what I did I could never please him. It was always something with him. He didn't like the way I played; I was never fast enough, could never keep up with him. He loved to boast his expensive equipment (although he failed to mention everything he owned was Dr. Mommy-and Daddy-bought), and would never fail to tell you he was better than you in every sense. If you took him apart, he wasn't much more than a spoiled rich kid trying to stand out in a family who gave too much, but loved too little.

Then there was Shelly. I guess I have to talk about her. Shelly was Steve's longtime girlfriend, which was why she tagged along with us from city to city selling our merchandise (we only sold one shirt with *Rot in Hell* printed on the front and *Loves your mom!* on the back) and occupied the middle row of the van by herself. She wasn't the best looking girl I had ever laid eyes on, nor was she the ugliest, but when you're stuck in a metal tube with nothing but sweaty guys, just about anything started to look good.

I knew from the start she had it in for me. She had laid it on thick, never once passing a moment away from Steve without letting me know she wanted me.

I know that sounds completely pretentious, but after being with Steve for nearly six years she obviously wanted some kind of change, and when I came into the picture my name immediately became Change.

Last—and certainly least—was D-Rail. I wish I could tell you I was friends with someone else other than Vinnie, someone I could relate with that wasn't necessarily a musician and could stand beside me in my annoyance of everyone. D-Rail was definitely not it. At six-foot-four, the guy scared the shit out of me. He almost never spoke, and seemed to have this uncanny ability to stand right behind you without you knowing it, then wait for you to turn around. I'm not sure if he thought it was funny creeping up on you like that, or if it was his only way of getting attention, but it always worked. Like Shelly, I often found him staring at me for long periods of time...but unlike Shelly he didn't use his *fuck-me* eyes. And the name D-Rail? I wasn't sure where it came from. I just figured his name was Darrel or something, and that just wasn't cool enough for him.

So there we were: Six individuals traveling the open road for one goal, but everyone had a different way of getting there.

Me?

I just wanted out.

***

Sweat hung thick in the air. It was the pungent aroma of packed-in bodies, unwashed pits, and greasy hair—the after-smell of a rock concert. A smell I knew all too well. My dad had taken me to many concerts as a child, only further advancing my love of music. The local stadium had been a place of inspiration, a house of worship. I saw that stadium as the apex of my future, my own Mt. Everest to conquer. I dreamed of one day standing just behind the curtains, guitar strapped over my shoulder, the crowd beyond clapping and stomping their feet, chanting *DAH-DAH-DAH* (insert band name here). My nerves would flare, fingers would tingle, pick slick with sweat. The lights suddenly go down. The crowd roars with suspense. And then—

That's where the dream dies.

I wasn't going anywhere with this band. Sure, they dreamed big—what band doesn't? What group of musicians doesn't strive for the collective purpose to sign their names on the dotted line? To tour with the top acts in your genre? To woo the girls? To buy all the ridiculous shit no one in their right minds would ever need until you had the money to waste on it? All pipe dreams for a bunch of mid-western twenty-something's in a white Ford van going nowhere.

Everything has its own smell. So does failure.

Another show had ended, and I retired to the back table of the barroom as I always did. The further away the better. Post-show privacy was all I desired, and those few short hours a night before we packed up and headed out was all I got. It looked like every other bar we'd ever played: various neon beer lights, scarred tabletops, minimal lighting. That evening surprised me, though. On a typical night we could count on an average of six to ten people waiting for us to play, but when we strapped on and stepped out we were all a bit shocked. Maybe Les' internet connections were finally paying off because, although I didn't exactly perform a head count, there were nearly fifty, maybe sixty people chanting *ROT-IN-HELL!*

As exciting as it was that maybe this band was gaining some steam, nothing could make me want to stay. You see, Vinnie and I were out. Well…not yet, but we were well on our way. We both had, in many ways, grown tired of the group. Although he was gung-ho at the beginning, I gradually watched him wear down to a nub. With Vinnie, it wasn't necessarily the music he was unhappy with, like it was for me, but more so the traveling. Like myself, he'd never been in a traveling band; I think the furthest he'd ever played away from home was three counties over. I watched Vinnie (who at the time I considered my closest friend, maybe my only friend) despond further into his own hell.

I wondered if he saw me the same way.

We had a plan, you see? The next day we would be pulling back into Evansville, then Vinnie and I would wave our goodbyes. For a while we were talking about starting our own group—but definitely not metal. We were tired of that. We wanted something different for a change, maybe something a little more funk-oriented. Did I know how to play funk? No. But I could damn sure learn.

How would the others take it? Who cared?

With a half-eaten, complementary pizza and two nearly empty beer mugs splayed across the table, I had laid my head down to rest. My stomach groaned, full.

I smelled her before I saw her.

"What is it now, Shelly?" Her vanilla body cream invaded my nostrils. She knew I liked it.

"I want to talk," she whispered.

My head swam. I wasn't quite drunk enough for this. "Go…away."

"Spence, we need to talk."

"Goddamn it, Shelly, I don't want to talk! I've made that pretty clear. That's why I sit away from everyone after our shows. That's why I sit in the back of the van. That's why I've told you time and again that you need to leave me alone—and yet here you fucking are, pestering me. What, Shelly? What could possibly be troubling you, my dear? What?"

For several moments Shelly was silent. I thought she would leave. "I want to talk about...us."

Shit.

I sat up and opened my eyes, a bit surprised to find her in the chair right next to me. She knew better than that, but from the way she was sitting and with the tiniest hint of a smirk, she was a woman on a mission. Yet again my name changed to 'Mission.' From my peripherals the rest of the group was sitting at a table not too far off. Steve sat in a backwards chair, shirtless, with his massive back tattoo that stuck out like a spinning red light. If you were trying to convey to the world you were a bad ass rock singer, I would not imagine that a white feathered cartoon duck with fisted hands on its hips and a massive hard dick would be your bag, but that's what the crowds got an eye-full of every night.

None of this mattered. Though I wanted to scream at Shelly's blatant recklessness in her affections, I found for a moment I couldn't speak. Her beauty caught me off guard, as she had intended. I found over the last six months she did just about anything she could to get my attention. She began wearing her hair down instead of spiked out, let the neon pink drain back to her natural straight golden locks. She took away the piercings and the extra clothing that covered her curves to bring forth the effortless beauty lying beneath. I was speechless for not one, but two reasons. One: the aforementioned sights. And two: she didn't fucking care who saw.

The anger came back quickly.

"You've got some balls, you know that, right?"

"Spence, you can't hide from me forever," she said,

leaning back with her arms crossed. "Sooner or later we're going to have to talk about, you know, us."

I wanted to snap. "There is no *us*, Shelly. There never was and never will be."

Her eyes narrowed. "I beg to differ, lover boy. What was it that you said two nights ago in Kansas City? Remember what you whispered in my ear when you were balls-deep in my ass in your hotel shower? I think it was something like 'I love you.'"

I smirked. "Most men utter such things when nearing orgasm."

Anger flash quickly over her eyes, but her features immediately softened. She leaned close, reaching out to touch my leg. "Spencer Hesston, why do you say such things? I—"

I smacked her hand away before she could touch me. Even though Steve had his back to me, the thought of him seeing her lay a hand on me was almost too much. And if he wasn't watching, then D-Rail probably was.

"Keep your hands off me. If Steve sees us even near each other he's going to shit a brick!" I didn't have to mention to her how he beat the hell out of the guy in Milwaukee for groping her in the audience.

"At this point," she countered, "I couldn't give a shit. And as far as I'm concerned, Steve and I have been done for quite some time, so keep your righteous bullcrap to yourself, Spence. You're everything that Steve's not, and that's why we fit so well."

I couldn't argue with that.

She continued, "I'm done sneaking around like this. I'm sick and tired of hiding every time I want to see you... I want to do it without the fear of getting caught by *him*. I love you."

"You don't love me, Shelly," I groaned. "You love the idea of me—the fact that I'm someone new and exciting, and you're getting off on the thrill of almost getting caught. So please, just get over it. We are not a couple, nor will we ever be." I figured that would shut her up.

Her eyes narrowed. "I know about you and Vinnie."

That got my attention. "Oh you do, do you? What is it you think you know?"

"I know you and Vinnie are quitting soon—hell, probably tomorrow when we roll back into home."

"You don't know shit," I growled.

"Ah, I can hear by your tone of voice I'm not too far off from the truth. So what is it? You two quitting and staying home to play in some junky bar band? Whatever. I don't care. All I know is that if Steve found out about this early, well…I can tell you he wouldn't be too pleased. Not at all."

I stood up, fuming. "Eat shit, Shelly." Leaving my food behind, I grabbed my beer and stomped over to where my band mates were collected.

As I sat down across from Vinnie, I couldn't help but wonder who else knew, and who told? I obviously didn't, so that only left Vinnie. I didn't want to believe our drummer would have told anyone our little secret—especially not so close to our departure—but with a few drinks in him there was no telling. For the moment, I suspected everyone was in on it, and I studied their expressions as I sat down. Steve was turned in his chair speaking to someone who came to see us play. Vinnie and Les were chatting (although Les kept glancing over at me). I caught D-Rail glaring. I turned away.

Done talking, Steve turned back to face everyone. "Well, howdy, stranger! Nice of you to come visit us."

My face crinkled. "Great to be here." Maybe Steve knew, about Shelly or us leaving, but for the moment

I didn't care.

Shelly pulled out the chair next to Steve, but kept a distance.

"Hey, babe. Where you been?" he asked.

Her eyes never left mine. "Around."

"We sell any shirts?"

"A few." She produced a lump of bills from her pocket and handed everyone their cut of the shirt money. When she came to me, she wadded the bills and tossed them at my face. A couple of ones and a single two dollar bill.

"Damn, boy," Steve croaked. "What did you do to deserve that?"

I quickly pocketed the cash, rolling my eyes.

Steve clapped his hands, begging for everyone's attention. "Alright, fuckheads, I'm holding the talking stick, so listen up!"

"You're holding your dick, bitch!" Les snorted.

"Your mom's holding my dick, fat boy. Now that I have your attention, I want to say something to you lovely bunch of coconuts. This has been a very long tour, brothers, a *very* long, invaluable, advantageous tour." Steve leapt up on his chair and waved his arms to and fro. The bartender stacking chairs in the corner was visibly annoyed. "We started our journey out on the Golden Coast, a whippin' and a thrashin', showing those stuck-up, kale eating West Coaster's how we fucking do it in the Midwest! We showed the Great White North how to keep their farmer's daughters warm on those snowy Canadian nights. 'I don't know what I've been told…'"

"But Eskimo pussy is mighty cold!" Les finished.

"Right on! We told Chicago their lasagna pizza sucks! We told New York to 'Get the fuck outta here!' We stuck a spurred boot up Texas' ass! And we showed that dick-shaped Florida we can take the whole length of that state and ask for more! And do you know why?"

The group, other than myself, roared, "*Why, Steve?*"

"Because we're Rot In Hell, motherfuckers!" he cried to a mostly empty bar. He hopped back down and leaned over the table. "We're the baddest bunch of white trash, middle-American metalheads you're ever going to come across. I'm proud of each and every one of you. Yes, even you, D-Rail, you creepy fuck." Steve clapped the big man's back. "Say something, you Lurch-looking motherfucker. Don't you ever talk?"

D-Rail simply showed a thumbs up to the table.

"Eh, whatever, D. Go back to eating small children in a dark cave somewhere." Steve raised his mug of beer, urging us to do the same. "Put 'em up. You are my brothers and my sister...although you can't be my sister, Shelly, because sisters don't blow their brothers." The table chuckled.

"Get on with it, Steve," Vinnie yelled. He was clearly over it, much like me.

"Yes, sorry. Where was I? Oh yes. You are all my brothers and sisters, and I want to continue this journey with you all for the rest of my whiskey-soaked life. Look, I know we're beat and broke, and I know we roll back into town tomorrow for a much needed break, but...don't bother unpacking. I'm proud to announce that I have booked us as the opening act for The Bowling Green Massacre and The Walls, They Bleed on their co-headlining European tour! And the best part,"—he slapped the table—"is that it starts next Wednesday in Brighton! That's in motherfucking England, boys!"

Everyone not named Spencer or Vinnie whistled and downed what was left in their mugs. My arm dropped back down to the table.

Les, nearly electric with excitement, screamed, "How did you make this happen? I mean, are you kidding me? The Bowling Green Massacre? That's crazy!"

"Because I'm the shit!"

Shelly hugged Steve around the neck and kissed his cheek, but her eyes never left me. "Seriously, Steve, this is so exciting! I've always wanted to go to Europe."

Steve pulled a face and gently pushed his girlfriend away. "Yeah, about that, babe…"

"What? What's wrong?"

"We, uh, can't afford to take you."

Shelly sat back down in her chair, eyes wide. "Excuse me?"

"I've already hammered out the details with the management of the other two acts, and the money just isn't there to take any more than the band and D-Rail."

Crossing her arms, Shelly's words sizzled. "Oh, so you can afford D, but not me? Is that what I'm hearing? Are you fucking kidding me?"

Steve threw his arms in the air. "Of course we have to take him! Unlike you, the budget is tight as hell. They're going to let us sell our merch at their table with their people, but they're not going to provide us with a driver. I mean, who else is going to drive our bus for next to nothing? Ain't that right, Swamp Thing?"

D-Rail shrugged, uninterested.

Bus? I laughed. *We'll be lucky to have a '76 Pinto to drive around in on Steve's budgets.* Steve's idea of saving money was never staying in hotels unless absolutely necessary and dining on room temperature ham sandwiches in the van between gigs. I wanted no part of this shit anymore. I stole a quick glance at Vinnie who I knew was thinking the exact same thing.

He sighed, shrugged, slammed down the rest of his beer, then pulled his cell out to check his Twitter.

Yep. Done.

But part of me wondered... Europe was awfully intriguing. As painful as it was to admit, getting to tour with two much bigger bands on bigger stages with bigger audiences was almost too good to be true. I wasn't all that familiar with The Walls, They Bleed— only by name—but I did however know The Bowling Green Massacre pretty well. They were up and coming, the next Lamb of God- or Shadows Fall-type, and very popular. The exposure alone...

No. I wouldn't let it distract me from what I truly wanted. *Just get through the next few hours and you'll be home and you'll never have to see these fucks ever again. Finding a new guitarist and drummer before next week is their problem, not yours. I'm sure it won't take long to learn a bunch of d-tuned chug sixteenth riffs.*

"Enough!" Lashing out, Steve grabbed Shelly by the cheeks, squeezed and threw her head to the side, nearly toppling her from her chair. "This is not the time or the place to discuss this with you!"

The table went quiet. Shelly grabbed her mouth and glared.

He continued, almost growling, "We will discuss this at home."

She nodded, then looked to me, then looked away.

"Great, Shelly. Thanks for the 'Daddy just hit Mommy at the dinner table' vibe. This is supposed to be a happy occasion, God damn it! We landed a once in a lifetime gig. I did that! For us! You all should be sucking my cock right now."

"I'm happy, Steve," Les said.

"You, see, Zach Galifianakis over here is happy to

gargle my bag! I'm sure Herman Munster over here is excited if he actually had human emotions. What about you, Vinnie? What say you, Kim Jong-un?"

Vinnie looked up from his phone, glaring, and gave a thumbs up. "Dilly Dilly." Under his breath he muttered, "Racist fuck."

"Very nice." Steve turned to me. "And you, Spence? What say you, pretty boy?"

I stared long and hard at my frontman, only wishing I could say half the things I really wanted to say. Better to just give him what he wanted and not start a scene in a biker bar in East St. Louis.

"Couldn't be more excited, Steve."

Steve paused before saying, "Good. Very good."

I suddenly surprised myself. "But I will tell you one thing. If you ever touch Shelly like that again—hit her, grab her face, whatever—I'll fucking end you. No ifs, ands, or buts. Understand?"

Steve crossed his arms, looking impressed. "Duly noted, pretty boy."

"OK then." Les stood, rolling his eyes. "I'm going to take a piss, then we need to get going. Still have a two and a half hour drive home."

"Yes, we do," Steve proclaimed. He turned to the bartender on the other side of the room. "Yo, bar wench, another round for the road!"

Les added, "And two more for the walk out to the van!"

***

I'll be perfectly honest with you: I truly don't remember what happened after we left Pop's Nightclub. I recall jumping into the van with a couple of cold six packs and some joints that we were gifted by a fan after the show, and then we directed ourselves onto I-64 East through Illinois and into Indiana.

Home.

With my freshly charged MP3 player buried in my ears, I took my spot in the back, then lit up some bud and closed my eyes...

When I would wake, we would be home.

Sadly, this wasn't the case.

March 13th (?)

"What the fuck!"
 I immediately sat up straight. Heart caught in my throat, my first groggy thought was I must have fallen asleep and set the damn van on fire. I shook my head and scrambled to find it. Fortunately I located the half-smoked joint burnt out, lying on a stained, soggy tube sock. Not sure what the liquid was that put it out, but I was thankful for it.
 "Where are they?" The voice made me jump again, and even though I knew it was Les, I had never in the short while I had been his bandmate heard him so manic. "God damn it, where are they?"
 I was alone in the van. Though I couldn't see the rest of the group, I could hear shuffling and mumbling near the equipment trailer outside. What I could see however was the blinding sunlight that seemed to rip right through the tinted windows like they weren't even here. I moaned, hungover and still a bit stoned, and found my sunglasses next to the dirty tube sock.
 The heat outside nearly choked me when I slid the side door open—*Too damn hot for August*, I thought—but what really caught me off guard was the sand. I expected my feet to hit pavement or grass, but I nearly fell to my ass when they sunk down in dry, hot grit. "What the hell?"
 Steve stepped around the back of the equipment trailer. "Rise and shine, Sleeping Beauty. Care to come around back here and explain this?"
 "Explain what?"
 He pointed toward the trailer.
 I sighed and gingerly walked through the sand to join the rest of the group. Each one wore the same dumbfounded expression. "Good morning," I croaked

and coughed. I could barely keep my eyes open behind my shades. "Hot as hell out here. Where are we? What's the matter?"

Les overexcitedly jabbed his hands out into the open trailer. "What the fuck do you think?"

I turned and quickly realized his actions were not unfounded.

Our equipment was gone.

The drums, the PA system, the merch, boxes of strings, guitars, amps...all gone. *They took the Who-pudding, they took the roast beast!*

Les seized me by my shirt with both fists and shook me. "Where's my Thumb, mother fucker?" (referring to his Warwick brand Thumb-style bass) "Where is it?"

I could barely breathe. I was just as confused as he was, maybe more. "I have no clue, Les! Get your fucking hands off me!" I tried to brush him off, but he tightened his grip.

"My Thumb! My Ampeg SVT-VR and cab! My pedal board! What did you do to them?"

I had no choice. Les was hysterical and on the verge of doing something stupid, and I was tired and felt sick to my stomach, so I beat him to it. I reached back and socked him in the gut—not too hard but enough to get him off me. Shelly gasped, and Vinnie quickly rushed to pull me back from hitting our distraught bassist again. Steve stepped between us.

"That'll be enough of that."

"What did you do with my shit, Hesston?" Les screamed, holding his stomach.

"What are you talking about, you dumb fuck?" I yelled back. "My shit is gone too! Everyone's shit is gone!" My anger quickly turned to sadness. My beloved Les Paul...gone. When I was sixteen I scrimped and saved every dollar I had. Cutting lawns all summer, birthday cash, allowances, selling a bit of weed here and there, got me my dream guitar. The same one my heroes Ace Frehley and Zakk Wylde played. The amps and pedals were replaceable, but the guitar was not. And just like Les's precious Warwick, it was gone. I wanted to cry.

"Where's all our stuff, Steve?" Vinnie asked.

Hands clasped behind his head, Steve stared into the empty black cavern of the trailer, his wide eyes searching for an answer.

"Steve!"

"I... Fuck! I don't know! D? Isn't it your responsibility to make sure the trailer is filled, secured and properly locked up before we leave every gig?"

D-Rail nodded.

"Well? Did you lock the fucking thing up or what?"

Again he nodded.

Frustrated, Steve growled and kicked the trailer door.

"Calm down, Steve," Shelly intervened. "I'm sure there's a reasonable explanation for this."

Steve whipped around like an angry rattlesnake and stomped toward her. "And what would that be? *Hmmm?* Is someone just borrowing our equipment and will politely bring it back when they're done? Wake up, you dumb bitch. Someone stole our shit!"

"Who are you calling a dumb bitch, you dumb bitch!"

Vinnie screamed, "Everyone please stop yelling and let's try to figure this out."

"My fucking Thumb, man..." Les moaned.

I had stopped paying attention. As pissed as I was about my rig being pinched, I was more focused on the sand covered road we were currently baking on. I wiped the sweat off my sunglasses and really focused on the surrounding area.

Other than our van, we were the only occupants of a narrow road that lead out into a small town just ahead of us, and behind us the road disappeared into the sun-caked horizon. It was only then I looked past both sides of the road.

"You guys?"

The crew continued to call each other all forms of bitch and mother fucker before I lost my patience. I turned and kicked sand at Steve and Shelly until they shut up, then pointed past the van.

"What the hell?" Vinnie mumbled.

The midday sun sat far beyond the miles of untouched desert before us, heat waves dancing over the untouched dunes. No trees, no bushes or rocks. Other than the town up the road, it was golden granules as far as the eye could see. The air was still and suffocating. Not a scaly creature in sight.

Steve asked, puzzled, "Why didn't I see that before?"

"You were too busy howling at each other to notice," I said.

Les finally broke from his stupor. "Where the hell are we?"

"We're definitely not in Missouri anymore." Vinnie added. "Outside of a playground, I'm not sure sand exists in the Midwest."

"Only up Shelly's twat," Steve said.

I wanted to drop down to my knees in frustration, but instead fell back against the blistering sidewall of the van. I just wanted to be home. With my parents. And my cat Ozzy. In my bed. Take a shower. Never touch a ham sandwich for as long as I lived. Instead, I found myself between whiney assholes and a barren desert. Then it hit me.

I quickly threw the side door back open and crawled

into the back row for my cell phone. I could call my dad, see if he maybe knew where we were—at the very least pull up the GPS app and find our location... wherever the hell that might be. But I couldn't find it. I checked under the seat, between the cushions, in the cup holder, even poked at the tube sock. Nada.

I snatched my backpack off the floor and opened it, thinking maybe I woke up at some point and shoved it in.

The whole thing was empty.

I sat back in my seat, dumbfounded. "My stuff is gone."

Vinnie poked his head in the van. "What?"

"All my electronics. Phone, laptop, MP3 player. All gone."

"Are you shitting me?"

I lifted my backpack upside down.

"No, no, no!" He leapt to his seat and grabbed his knapsack. "Fuck! My shit's gone too! Cell phone, books, drum pad, all of it."

The backdoor creaked open and the van was suddenly filled with oppressive sunlight. "Where are our clothing bags?" Shelly yelled.

Steve punched the van door. "For fuck's sake."

"How does this even happen?" Les was nearly in tears.

"We got robbed, crybaby. It's pretty damn obvious."

"Everything's gone in the van, Steve," Vinnie said. "Everyone's bags are empty. No cells either."

Steve paced and ran his hands through his greasy hair. "Are the keys still in the ignition?"

Vinnie hopped into the front seat for a few moments, then came back empty handed. "Unfortunately not."

Laughing, Steve rounded the front of the van and threw the driver's side door open. He hysterically searched for the keys, throwing loose papers and candy wrappers into the air. Vinnie rolled his eyes.

"*FUCK!*" He repeatedly punched the steering wheel. The horn beeped with every strike.

"Steve, stop," Shelly yelled. "We all need to calm the hell down and figure out where we are and how his happened."

"Agreed," I said. I took a deep breath, trying to will the fogginess in my brain to dissipate. "Let's start from last night, OK?"

Knuckles red and raw, Steve sat back and sighed. "Fine. We left the bar around twelve…forty-five, correct?"

Everyone nodded.

"We distributed a few drinks and joints to everyone and then got onto the road, correct?"

Again we nodded.

"Then we…"

"What?" Vinnie asked.

Steve paused, staring straight ahead. "I don't remember."

"What do you mean you don't remember?"

Steve turned to face him. "I mean what I said: I don't remember. All I remember is sitting in the front seat with my beer and the next thing I know I'm waking up to Les hollering bloody murder out back."

I asked, "Was Les the first to wake up?"

Kicking sand, Les said, "I-I-I-don't know. I guess so."

"You guess so? Was everyone else asleep when you woke up?"

"Yes."

"Did you see anyone? Anything at all?"

Les ran his hands through his long, black hair, tears rolling down his cheeks into his beard. "No. I just woke up and realized we were stopped. I needed to take a leak, so I stepped outside and noticed the equipment trailer door was open."

"You swear you didn't...wait, why were we stopped?" I turned to D-Rail, who was standing just outside the sliding door, staring out into the desert. "D? Why were you sleeping?"

D-Rail turned back with a blank expression.

"Why did you pull over? To sleep?"

He stared at me and blinked.

"Hello?" I yelled. "Anything rattling around in that empty fucking skull of yours?"

He didn't answer, only turned back to face the sunlight.

"Oh, for fucks sake." From day one, D-Rail hated me. Though he never actually spoke to me personally I knew he couldn't stand me. The feeling was mutual.

Shelly spoke up. "You guys, that guy that gave us the weed? Maybe he, like, laced it with something and then followed us and waited for us to pass out then robbed us?"

Steve laughed, "I've smoked plenty of herb, and that shit we had was skunk weed at best. There was nothing in it, other than maybe some oregano for filling."

"And even if that was the case," Vinnie added, "that doesn't explain how we got here, wherever *here* is."

"The beer, man!" Les yelled. "I'll bet that fucking bartender spiked the beer he gave us before we left!"

I yelled back, "Nobody spiked anything, you overdramatic fuck!" My head pounded. I needed some fresh air. "Look, there's a town just up the road. Why don't we head up there and see if we can find a phone or a bite to eat and figure this out. I'm sure there's a reasonable explanation for all of this."

"Good idea," Shelly said. She grabbed Steve's shirt sleeve and urged him down from the front seat. Les and D-Rail followed behind, and Vinnie and I were a deliberate distance behind them.

Sweat dripped down my forehead into my eyes. "Jesus Christ, Vinnie."

"I know, man. I can't believe our stuff is gone. That Tama drum set cost me well over a grand, not to mention those cymbals. Shit's expensive."

"I'm sorry, bud. So did my Les Paul." I started to get sad again, so I decided to cheer myself up a bit. "So I was thinking about potential band names..."

Vinnie glanced at me with a crooked smile. "Really? That's the last thing I want to think about right now."

"Come on. I know this sucks, believe me, but I'm not going to sulk the entire time. Hey, we're free men. The tour's done. We're no longer in Rot In Hell."

He nodded toward the others. "Do they know that yet?"

"Fuck 'em. We'll tell them when we get back to town."

A grin grew across his face. "We are free, aren't we?"

"Yes, sir. And now we are officially the founding members of Earthworm Gods."

"Earthworm Gods? Sounds like a title to some shitty horror book."

I thought about it. "Yeah, I think it is. OK, here's a better one: Carpet Fudge."

Vinnie laughed out loud. "*Carpet Fudge?*"

"Hell yeah. Sounds great for a funk band, right? Very sixties."

"Is that what we're going to play? Funk?"

"My man," I said, placing my arm around his shoulder, "We can play whatever we want."

***

Silent doesn't begin to describe how quiet the town was. The six of us walked slowly down the sandy road until we reached a packed dirt street that led into the town's opening. It was like stepping into an old spaghetti western. Large two and three story buildings lined both sides of the street, most of varying businesses, painted in assorted sunburnt shades of white and gold. They almost looked fake, like we had stumbled onto a movie set, and the backs of the buildings were nothing more than two-by-fours holding up a flat, decorated wall for some cowboy to lean against. We passed a barber shop and shoe repair store and a couple of dress shops, all of their windows caked with dirt.

And all empty.

Our footsteps echoed off the building fronts. I motioned for everyone to stop.

Steve asked, "Where is everyone?"

"Shhhh," I said.

We stood there quietly, listening for...anything really. I figured we had stumbled into some old timey mining town, the kind people stopped at while driving across country to the beach with their kids. Moms would try on overpriced frilly dresses, and Dads would find a saloon for cold beer in warm mugs. Everyone would get their pictures taken by the gallows and leave, completely forgetting they even went to the tourist trap until a house guest comments on the framed photo in the hallway.

It was dead silent.

My stomach gurgled, and the sound reverberated back to me. I hadn't realized how hungry I was until my body started speaking up. While searching for a restaurant, I noticed just how empty the town was, and just how alone we were. I hadn't seen a single tire or even animal track since we'd arrived. Hell, I hadn't even seen a tumbleweed stuck to a horse post yet. It was a strange feeling, being somewhere that noiseless. Being a musician means a constant assault on the senses. If music isn't being played, then people are screaming. The trundling and creaking of the van. A musician is constantly in their heads, sounds and riffs ever-forming. Never a minute goes by where you're not focusing on something creative, but the desert heat killed every thought I had.

"Christ, I'm thirsty," Steve mumbled.

"We all are," I said.

"HELLO?" We jumped at Les' yell.

"Come on, man."

"What? I'm fucking hot and I'm tired of walking, and if anyone's here they're certainly not going to hear us just by your rumbly tummy."

He had a point. Collectively we called out for help, each of us at varying volumes (other than D-Rail, who just stood there silently like a complacent dog). For some reason it felt strange to me to bellow at the top of my lungs. The whole place felt off, and it unnerved me we hadn't seen a single shred of life. I wasn't positive I wanted to meet anyone who actually made this type of place their home.

Their cries for help continued, but were only answered by their echoes. "Alright, enough," I lamented. They stopped, visibly frustrated. We were all drenched in sweat, and the sun didn't seem to give in to our cries. If anything it felt hotter. We needed to find shelter.

"You guys, I think we're alone here."

Steve laughed. "Really? What gave you that impression, Hesston?" By now Steve had taken off his tank top, giving everyone a look at that eyesore on his back.

"Look, it's obvious we're in the middle of fucking nowhere. I'm not in the mood to fight or argue. It's too hot. I'm hungry and tired and I don't feel like trudging through this sandy hellhole anymore. Let's just find a place that's open and go from there. Agreed?"

We settled on a side street and quickly came across a small row of what looked like residential homes. At one point they would have been beautiful had time and the elements not stripped them of personality. Paint was long gone, leaving only dry, rotted wood frames that bent to the sun's will. There were four houses on each side of the street, all nearly identical: three stories, columned porches, small picket fences bordering sand covered lawns. The end of the street opened up to the endless sand dunes.

I followed Vinnie up to the first house while Shelly and Steve went to the house next door. Les and D-Rail watched us dumbly from the street. Vinnie quietly knocked on the door and we waited for any response. "Hello?" I asked. Our drummer knocked again, a bit louder, but no one answered. I walked across the porch and pressed my face against the front picture window but the glass inside was so caked with filth on the inside I couldn't make anything out.

Across the yard, Steve banged the neighbor's front door with a tight fist. "Hello? Anyone there? Open up, I need to take a shit!"

"Christ, Steve," I yelled. "You're going to scare them."

"Scare who? There's no one here. There's no one anywhere." He then nudged Shelly out of the way, stepped back and kicked the door. With little resistance the door swung inward and smacked the wall inside.

"Little pigs, I'm coming in." He disappeared into the house.

"For fucks sake." Vinnie and I joined the others as they walked up the creaky wooden steps and into the house.

***

Sorry about that. Didn't mean to leave you. After I finished that last part, I went to close my eyes for a rest, not realizing it would turn into an extended nap. I've never been a big fan of naps. I always seem to wake up sweaty and disoriented…not unlike how I woke in the van. That 'Holy fuck, I'm late for work!' feeling.

Sorry. I'm stalling. You don't deserve that. You deserve to know the truth. Everything's been easy to write out thus far.

The rest going forward?

Not so much.

***

My brain told me someone, some pissed off husband with a family to protect, would be waiting for us on the other side to tear us in half with a shotgun, or at the very least a bunch of bums, squatting and using the floors as a toilet. All we found was a bunch of ancient, dust covered furniture.

The couches and cabinets were caked in a half an inch of soil and grime, as was the floor. It was much cooler in the house, which was a major relief, because the windows too were heavily covered but with rags and shreds of paper. Only slivers of sun snuck through to give us light. The couches appeared dated and worn, untouched for some time if ever, but that didn't stop me. A quick wipe of the cushion and I plopped my tired frame down. Vinnie joined me, while Les and Shelly took the adjacent love seat. Steve paced the house, looking for a phone or food. D-Rail stood in the corner and glared.

I sighed. "So what now?"

In the next room over Steve rummaged through cabinets and cursed out loud as he slammed them shut. "Nothing going in here. Not a goddamn thing anywhere. Cabinets, refrigerator—both empty." He stepped back into the living room, sweat rolling down his bare chest. "Doesn't look like this place has been occupied in years, maybe ever."

Shelly asked, "So then where are we? What is this place, this town?"

"I don't know, Shelly. I don't have an answer for you. Maybe it's, like, a nuclear test site or something, like in that Hills Have Eyes flick?"

"Well, someone has to know. I refuse to believe that we were in Missouri and woke up in the southwest or something. It's not possible."

"I agree," I added. "It just doesn't seem likely."

Steve threw his hands in the air. "Well, it's obviously possible. We're here, aren't we? We just need to figure out where here is."

"Maybe you should ask that dumbass duck on your back where we are," Vinnie mumbled.

Steve twisted his back to us, showing his erect cartoon fowl. "What say you, Mr. McDuck? Are we in Flagstaff again? What's that? Vinnie's a chink and should keep his mouth shut? Hmmm, I agree."

Vinnie quickly shot up from his seat and balled his fists. "The fuck did you just say to me?"

"Calm down, Short Round. It was a joke."

"I'm sorry, racism is a joke to you? You got a

problem with me being Korean?"

Steve stepped up to challenge him. "I said calm down, Long Duk Dong. It was a joke."

Goddamn it. I quickly got between them. "Enough."

"No, Spence, it's never enough," Vinnie growled. "I'm sick of this dickhead name-calling and picking and grinding on everyone's nerves. I've had it."

Steve sighed. "Christ, you're such a baby."

"I'm a baby? Look at yourself, Steve. You're a living stereotype—the loud, brash metal singer, always the center of attention. Oh, I gotta have crazy tattoos and I can't stop talking about how much whiskey I drink or coke I snort or how many groupies I fuck."

I quickly exchanged glances with Shelly from across the room. Her eyebrow arched. "Excuse me?"

"Don't listen to him, hon. He's just mad he's always going to play second fiddle to someone like me. He's a fucking loser."

Vinnie attempted to push me out of the way, but I kept him in place. "You're a liar and a talentless hack. Why don't you tell your precious girlfriend about the twins in Jersey? Or that big ass redhead from Miami? Or that tranny chick you couldn't stop obsessing over in Reno? Remember her?"

Shelly approached her boyfriend, teeth gritted. "The fuck is he talking about, Steve?

Steve's face turned beat red. "If you value your teeth, Vincent, I suggest you keep your trap shut."

"Goddamn it, Steve!" Shelly screamed, yanking her boyfriend's hair. "What did you do?"

Everything happened so quickly. In a flash Steve turned and, with a *crack*, smacked Shelly right across the face. Before she hit the ground, I lunged and drove my fist into Steve's nose. Steve yelped and joined Shelly on the dusty floor. Heavy footsteps thumped across the floor and before I could react, D-Rails hands were around my throat. Though I'm not sure how high he lifted me, I no longer felt the floor. Les yelped and stood up from the love seat. Shelly crawled across the floor, away from Steve. Vinnie stepped away, unsure of what to do. I gagged as his fat, sausage-like digits squeezed into my neck. I too had no idea how to react.

"That's enough, D," Steve moaned as he stood up. Blood trickled down his nose over his lips.

D-Rail turned to look at Steve then dropped me. I collapsed, gasping for air. Before I could stand again, D-Rail was already back against the wall in the far corner of the room.

Steve blew his bloody snot onto the floor by Vinnie's feet. "You've got balls, Hesston, I'll give you that. You kept your word. I admire that. But I promise that's the last time that will happen. Try that again and I'll have D cut you down."

Vinnie shook his head, disgusted. "I'm done. I quit."

"You what?"

"I fucking quit. I'm done with this. It's one thing to name call and berate, it's another to attack your bandmates and your girlfriend. I've already lost my equipment and all my belongings, but I'm not losing my dignity too."

Steve appeared genuinely perplexed. "You *quit*? After everything I've done for you? For us? I just booked us a European tour, you slant-eyed fuck. I did that! Not you, you, you, you, or you. Me! You ungrateful little shit."

"Fuck the tour!" Vinnie screamed.

Somewhere I heard someone sniffing.

Shelly, keeping her distance, cried, "You son of bitch, I can't believe you hit me."

"You want me to do it again, bitch? Keep talking."

Suddenly I heard multiple noses sniffing. It started quietly, then got noticeably louder, in unison. I stood up, rubbing my throat. I noticed Les shaking his head at Vinnie and me.

"You're both traitors."

"Shut up, Les. Do you hear that?"

"Steve's right. You're both ungrateful. We have this once in a lifetime opportunity and you're going to piss it away? We can't find another drummer that quickly! Hell, I can't even afford to get new gear that quickly."

The sniffing got louder. Closer.

"This is all your fault, Spencer. I want my Thumb and my amp back!"

I put my hand up to shush him. "Do you guys here that?"

Steve took a step toward Vinnie. "All I hear is a fucking dead man."

"What's that noise?" Shelly asked.

"Where's our equipment, Spencer?" Les commanded.

I finally lost my patience. "*I don't have your mother fucking bass or your amp, you stupid bastard! I don't have any of it! Now will you please shut the fuck up!*"

The whole room went silent.

Now I could hear it clearly. Multiple noses, sniffing loudly, over and over.

Shelly asked, "What is that?"

"I don't...know." I answered.

Steve shrieked, giving us all a definitive answer. He threw himself against the wall.

A man—at least I thought it was a man—was crouched on the floor between Steve and Vinnie. He was completely nude, and his skin was as pallid and unblemished as a sheet of printer paper. He kept low to the floor, bald head down, slowly shuffling on his forearms and knees. Sniffing, he turned toward the wad of snotty blood on the floor. Vinnie took a step back and pressed himself against the dusty wall. Shelly gasped and stepped back with Les toward the front door. D-Rail took a tentative step forward, but Steve stopped him.

"What the hell is that?" Vinnie whispered.

I held my hand out toward him. "Don't move."

The man gradually inched toward the blood. As soon as he turned his body, he revealed a long, thick fish-like tail which protruded from his rear end. The appendage waved back and forth but turned ridged and vibrated as it approached the blood. He lowered his head and sniffed loudly, enthusiastic. Then he lifted his head and instantly became an *it*.

Its face was pale blank canvas, void of eyes and a nose and anything you would call human. Two small vertical slits served as its nose. It sniffed the air, then opened a small, puckered anus-like mouth and gave us a view of its glossy fangs. Across from the creature, Vinnie whimpered as he attempted to sidestep away. The creature whipped its head back and made a low gurgling sound in its throat. Simultaneously, Shelly and Les screamed, both pointing to the ceiling. I looked up.

Like bats, several more of the pale, fish tailed creatures were clustered just above Vinnie. Their tails and bodies vibrated like an incoming call. Before anyone could move, they dropped on Vinnie and smothered him, the floor creature hopping in to join them. Together they pinned him to the floor and sunk their fangs into his prone body. The five of us screamed, as did Vinnie, as the fanged creatures drained him. Behind me, I heard the front door bang open as Shelly,

D-Rail, and Les made a break for it. Steve broke from his paralysis and shouldered past me and out the door.

I couldn't move. Couldn't breathe. Could only watch as these *things* emptied my friend on the floor of a vacant house in the middle of sunbaked nowhere. I took a weary step forward. I wanted to help him, to yank him out from the dogpile—at the very least take a shot at one of those monstrosities—but the floorboard groaned under my foot.

The creatures immediately stopped slurping and turned right toward me. Blood dripped from their tight little lips. Underneath them, Vinnie had stopped moving. He was as pale as they were. In unison they stood, much taller than I had anticipated, and began sniffing in my direction.

"*Spencer!*" Shelly screamed from somewhere outside.

They moved toward me, and I finally made the right decision and fled.

***

Was it the right decision? This thought tends to keep me up a lot of nights. I can still see their eyeless faces and their pale, colorless bodies, the way they drank my friend. Strangely, Vinnie never made a sound. Before I ran, I swear I could almost see him smiling...

Sometimes I think I should have tried harder for him. Instead I pussed out like the others, those cowards, and ran for it. In the end it was probably for the best. I didn't want to die like that. As much as I hated the other four, I didn't want any of us to die. But there was much more out there for us. So much more.

Anyway, sorry. Got lost in my thoughts. Back to the non-fiction.

***

The amount of green that greeted me outside was assaulting. I nearly tripped at the top of the steps, but as I reached the bottom my foot twisted, and the ground rushed up to meet me. At that moment I wasn't thinking about how I may have hurt myself by falling or if anyone would help me up to see if I was alright (they didn't), or even if anyone was going to help Vinnie. I was wondering why my face was laying on grass.

I stood up, heart pounding, and began to run toward the street—but stopped dead in my tracks.

Steve, Shelly, Les and D-Rail stood silently on the other side of the fence, which was now overgrown with vines and various plant life. All around us the street, the town—the entire landscape—had changed. Gone were the decrepit wooden houses and the raw, coarse sand that surrounded them. The sun above was nearly swallowed by the massive tropical trees that dominated the street. What little light shown through illuminated the emerald jungle around us, as well as rich shades of red and blue that would have been stunning had I not been frozen in fear. I looked beyond the street to what was once a vast desert, finding only an endless sea of vines and undergrowth that became black at the end of my vison. My flesh prickled at the sudden absence of heat.

Slowly I walked off the lawn and joined the others in the street. Suddenly remembering the creatures, I turned to find the house we had just escaped was nearly sealed off by creeping ivy, and the front door was shut as though it was never open.

Vinnie, my only friend, was gone with the sand.

I felt bile rise in my throat. "Why didn't you help

him?" I turned away from the house. My ears burned. "Why the fuck didn't you help him?"

Steve could not look at me straight. His eyes continuously bounced back and forth from me to the trees to the house. "W-w-what? Help who?"

"Help who? *Help who?* Help Vinnie, you goddamn troglodyte! You left him to be bled dry by those—"

"Vampires," Les mumbled.

I shot him a glare. "They weren't vampires, Les. Vampires don't exist."

Shelly started to cry. She fell to her knees and buried her face into her chest. Part of me wanted to console her, but my anger was beyond that.

"Then what were they, Spence?" Steve asked. "What else bites someone with fangs and drinks their blood—and by the fucking way, how dare you accuse me of not helping Vinnie! I didn't see you move a muscle to stop them."

I growled, "I did try, you bastard! They turned and came after me! I couldn't do anything after that! Les, Shelly, and D did even less than you, which makes all of you cowards."

Shelly sobbed harder. Now I know I didn't want to touch her.

Steve threw his hands up, frustrated. "Look, what's done is done. Vinnie's gone, and he ain't coming back. As you can plainly see, we have bigger problems right now."

Vinnie's gone, and he ain't coming back. It was just that easy to Steve. Our drummer, my friend—my best friend—was nothing more than an ex-bandmate now, a footnote on a Wikipedia page, a future VH1 *Where Are They Now?* contender. Replaceable. I stumbled back to the fence for support and puked up last night's pizza onto the lawn.

I felt a hand drop on my shoulder. "Spence, I'm so, so sorry," Shelly cried.

I shrugged off her condolence. "Get the hell off me." I got back up and walked past her, not wanting to give her another moment of my time. If I had any feelings toward her, sexual or otherwise, they were very much gone. Her very essence disgusted me. How she could ever be with Steve, a man-child who used and abused her, made me sick. Her affections toward me, though perfectly understandable, were not reciprocated past physical activity. I no longer wanted to look at her.

I started to walk away from the others but stopped directly in front of D-Rail. "Got anything to say for yourself? You were good enough to choke me out but not enough to help Vinnie?"

D-Rail stared at me coldly with his chin up in the air.

"All muscle and no brains. I'm sure if Steve told you to jump you'd wiggle your ass until he said how high. Get the fuck out of my face." I stepped past him to walk back down the street to what was left of town.

"Where are you going?" Steve asked.

Without turning around, I answered, "I'm going back to the van."

"Why?"

I didn't answer. I just kept walking.

***

My intention was to get back to the van and wait. Wait for what? I had no idea, but I knew I didn't want to lay eyes on any of those four losers for as long as I lived. Maybe I was in the wrong, screaming and pointing fingers while one could have just as easily been pointed back at me, but the death of my friend made me understandably unreasonable. Up to that point the only death I had ever witnessed was when I was thirteen and our basset hound Jimmy Page was hit by a car in our cul-de-sac. I was supposed to be watching him while he went out to defecate. Instead I was on the phone, inside, buying concert tickets with my mother's credit card. That thump I heard froze me, and it's a sound that still echoed in my brain whether I wanted it to or not. Heartbroken, we got a cat shortly after. I named him Ozzy. I really missed that little gray and white cat right then.

Much like the small residential street behind me, the town center ahead had become a deep jungle of ferns, low hanging vines and dense vegetation. The building fronts, those shops, restaurants and bars, were concealed in a thick leafy flora that smelled as damp as it looked. Windows and doors smothered and sealed. I wanted to stop and try to reason with myself that none of this was actually happening, that it was impossible for an entire landscape to change in the matter of several minutes. Gold to green. Hot to cool. It was not probable. Yet there I was, expecting to be greeted by chimpanzees at any moment.

The jungle was uncomfortably silent.

I trudged through the growth, aware that no one was following me. I had no idea if they decided to stay back or go Indiana Jones-ing themselves through the underbrush, but I was thankful they didn't tail me. I kept a good pace, trying to remember exactly how to get back to the main road out of town. It was much easier before when I could read store fronts. Once I found the shoe repair place I knew I was on the right track. Eventually I found a clearing past the last two adjacent buildings and I spotted the van about a half-mile straight ahead. Overhead the sunlight shone down on the thick, drooping blades of untouched grass that stood perfectly still. Part of me did not want to step foot into the meadow. It was almost beautiful, serene.

I kept mindful as I approached our van. Even after all that had happened, we still had no idea where we were or how we got there. My skin prickled. I was suddenly very aware of how alone I was. I shivered and ran the last thirty or so feet. Unlike the rest of the town, the van had been virtually unmolested by the perplexing greenery. I raced toward it, slid the side door open, then hopped in and slammed the door shut and locked it.

For the first time in a long time, I was truly alone. Vinnie was gone, *really* gone, and I had no other friends or allies. Wherever we were, it was so far away from home. The tears were sudden, and they came strong and hard. I sat on the front bench and bawled until my eyes burned, and I could cry no more. My stomach heaved, but only foamy spit was produced.

Then I heard a buzz.

I froze, waiting for it to repeat. When it did I quickly hopped over the middle two rows until I reached my row in the back. My cell phone was there, by itself, as if I had left there to begin with. I knew for a fact I had not. Heart hammering, I searched outside the tinted windows but found no one spying on me. The incoming call from was from DAD. I swiped the screen and pressed it to my ear.

"Dad?"

"Spencer? Is that you?" He sounded panicked.

"Yes!" I nearly screamed. "Yes, it's me, Dad!"

He sighed, relieved. "Oh, thank God. I've been trying to get a hold of you for days. Where have you been?"

"Days? We just talked yesterday morning."

"Yesterday? What are you talking about, son? We haven't spoken in, what…three, four days now? You were still in Des Moines."

Three or four days? That can't be right. I specifically remember speaking to him yesterday while on the road to St. Louis from Kansas City. He told me about the banquet the city mayor was throwing for Mom in her honor. They were going to attend that night to celebrate her latest NASA mission and her past accomplishments. I was really sad I was not able to make the ceremony.

"Dad, listen, something really bad happened."

"Something bad? What happened, Spencer? Are you OK?" It was so comforting to hear his genuine concern.

"Yeah, I'm fine, Dad. But…" I started to choke up again. I took a deep breath. "Vinnie's dead, Dad."

There was a small pause before he responded. "Dead? What do you mean dead?"

I started to cry again, I couldn't help it. "I'm sorry."

"Listen to me, Spencer. Just calm down and tell me what happened. Slowly."

I wiped my eyes and took a few deep breaths. "OK, so last night we played at Pop's—remember that place where you took me to see Black Label Society several years ago?—and we left right after the show to finally come home for a while. I…I don't know what happened after that. We—and I'm sorry you have to hear this—smoked some weed and got drunk and somehow woke up in some random cow-poke town in the middle of nowhere, and all our stuff has been stolen, and we were attacked by these *things*, and Vinnie was killed, I think. I'm pretty sure he's dead. I got in a big fight with the others, and now I'm alone back in the van and I don't know what to do."

My father went quiet, and for a minute I was not

sure if he was still on the line. I waited for his response, an 'I'm so sorry, I'll come and get you,", "It's OK, bud, we'll figure this out together,", or at the very least a stern lecture on the dangers of drugs and alcohol (like I was not in my early twenties).

What I got was, "Well, maybe it's for the best."

I stiffened, unsure of what to say. "Ex...excuse me?"

"You heard me, Spencer. It's for the best. You and Vinnie were going to quit the band anyway, right? Isn't that what you told me before?"

I pulled the phone away from my face, disgusted. "What the fuck?"

"You're both a couple of conspiring traitors. You *want* the band to fail, don't you? You both did this knowing damn well you had an obligation to your other bandmates. You're both failures. He deserved to die."

My hand shook. "...Dad?"

"And you deserve to die too."

I wanted to puke again. This was not my father. This was not the man who bought me my first guitar and let me play his extensive album collection whenever I wanted. Even at his angriest or drunkest he never would have expressed such a thing. It shook me to my core. I then remembered he had the same type of cell phone as me. I hesitantly clicked the video call button and, chest throbbing, waited for the other end to accept.

The call screen went away and a dark silhouette greeted me on the other side. His face was slightly out of focus, just behind a veil of shadows. All I could make out was the vague shape of a head and shoulders and nothing more. On the small rectangular screen in the bottom right corner my face looked pale and terrified.

"Dad?"

"Yes, son." His voice had become deeper and alien to my ears.

"Why did you say those things?"

"Because you deserve to die, son. You all deserve to die." His voice continued to change and warp, as if two voices spoke the same words, one higher and one lower.

"Dad, where's Mom? I want to speak to Mom."

My father leaned forward to where only the tip of his nose showed in the light. "She's dead too. We're all dead, son."

I closed my eyes and swallowed. "Dad…where am I right now?"

He slowly tipped forward into the light.

"My boy, you are in Hell."

In full view he revealed a head and face that resembled melted candle wax. His sallow skin hung down over his eyes and lips, drooping over his chin like it was running from his bones.

I screamed. The phone in my hand, much like the face inside it, began to melt. I dropped the device and it hit the cushion in a mushy splash. After a few moments it was nothing more than another stain I had slept on.

I couldn't breathe. Suddenly it was far too claustrophobic in the van, and my body told me to get the hell out. I tried to stand, but my pants were stuck to the seat. Grabbing the seat in front of me, I used it to lift myself, but my ass would not budge. All around me the van groaned as it too began to melt. The windows and sidewalls liquefied like hot ice cream, and I knew if I did not get out I too would be slush. I pulled with all my strength until my jeans tore from the seat and I could crawl to the side door. I unlocked the door and slid it open. It fell straight off the hinges and splashed on the ground. I dove through and hit the grass outside. Before I could even stand, the van was already a pile of gray and white goop that bubbled in the center.

At that point I was through. I wanted nothing more of this. I wanted to wake up from this bad acid trip. At that moment, more than anything else, I did not want to be alone. Even if it meant being around those other four, I would stomach it until we found a way out of there. I turned and made a beeline for the edge of town and quickly found I did not have to look any further for company.

Hundreds of shapes stepped out from the rim of the jungle into the sunlight of the meadow. Though they walked sluggishly they did so with purpose. Right toward me.

Each one of them was my dad.

"We're all dead, son."

Like his face in the phone, they were all chanting in their two toned voice, and like the van they too were liquefying. Skin and organs shook and bounced with their uneven steps, and when they gave away they hit the large blades of grass with a sickening splash. As they got closer to me, their bones began to reach the surface. Yet they kept coming.

"We're all dead, son."

I grabbed my hair and screamed, not sure what to do. "Please stop!"

"We're all dead, son."

When they were close enough to smell, I knew I had no other choice. I ran for town or whatever was left of it. As I approached my closest father I grimaced, as there was not much left of him. At that point he was a living anatomical medical model: bones and cartilage gleaming behind raw dripping muscle.

"We're all de—"

I didn't want to hear it. I closed my eyes and pushed through, clotheslining him as I passed. I gagged as his head came clean off his shoulders. It popped and splattered the grass behind me.

***

Still with me? Just checking.

***

As far as I could tell they were not following me. By the time I reached the jungle's edge, I could guess there wasn't much of them left to follow. Though it sickened me, my imagination emitted a large, soupy misshapen pile of arms and legs crawling after me, begging me to soften with them. But I was alone once again.

The jungle swallowed my cries, and thankfully so. Fear and adrenaline took over, causing me to make sounds I had never made before. Though the heat was minimal, sweat poured down my face, obscuring my vison, giving me more reasons to cry out in fury. Vines and low hanging branches slapped at my face and cut my arms. They seemed to lean in my direction, aware of my distress. I tried to remember the path I had taken to the meadow, but the more I was struck the more I lost my drive and memory. Some sick part of me wanted to trip and fall and let the jungle absorb me. After seeing my father's skin flux from his body, I didn't know if I could continue on. I was reminded of poor Jimmy Page, and realized his death knell had officially been replaced.

Eventually I stumbled back into town and was surrounded by a somewhat recognizable situation.

Exhausted, I dropped to one knee in front of the shoe repair shop and waited for my breath to catch up. What I really wanted was to find a soft bed—even a pile of leaves would do—to lay down and fall asleep until this was all over, but I was hyper aware of what could happen if I did. Every time I blinked I was terrified of what would be there when I opened my eyes. When I finally stopped shaking, I stood and slowly crept back up near the building fronts. Though there was no telling what else I might run into, I did not desire to be out in the open where I could be seen.

When I reached the end of the block, I waited. For what, I wasn't sure. As much as my fingertips buzzed in anticipation, I had to keep moving. I really needed to see a familiar face, preferably one not melting. Above me, branches and leaves shook. I tried my best not to mind them. I was already scared and didn't need another reason to start running again. I balled my fists and walked with a brisker pace until I crossed the street.

Behind me feet shuffled.

That I could not ignore. I turned around just as a large white shape disappeared behind a tree. Heart hammering, I waited, expecting whatever it was to come out the other side. When it didn't reappear, I hissed out a sigh. I would have given anything for a weapon right then.

I turned back to the direction I was going, but halted.

Wood creaked and groaned as the trees all slowly turned in my direction. Deep in their trunks, ancient knotty eyes stared me down.

I froze, unsure of what to do. I held my breath waiting for something to happen, for them to pull their roots from the earth and shuffle toward me. But they remained in place, blinking with bark lids. They studied me, then looked to one another, then back at me. If anything, they looked terrified. Had I intruded on something? I took a small step backwards and caught another flash of the large white shape off to my right as it darted between two buildings. I quickly turned back to the trees, but they had become normal once more.

Out of options, I backed up and pressed my back against the front of a building, waiting for some idea of what to do to reveal itself. I did not have to wait long.

A hand clasped around my mouth.

I gasped and turned to fight but discovered the hand belonged to Steve. His finger was pressed to his lips, urging me to hush. Behind him Les, Shelly and D-Rail stood nervously quiet. I never heard them coming, which for some reason scared me more than the trees.

"Have you seen it?" Steve whispered, taking his hand off my face.

"Seen what?"

"I don't know what the fuck it is, but it's pretty damn big."

"If you're referring to that white thing that keeps playing hide and seek, yes, I've seen it, but only glimpses. What is it?"

"No idea," Les said, "and we don't want to find out." He looked like he was going to be sick. Underneath his beard, his face was drained of color.

Steve shoved me. "Where the fuck have you been?"

I gritted my teeth. "I went back to the van like I said I was going to, or don't you listen?"

"Bandmates don't abandon each other, dumb dick!" His voice got louder. "Friends don't run out because they're scared!"

"Oh, bandmates don't abandon one another? How

about how you left Vinnie to die? Didn't seem to mind running out like a scared little bunny then, huh? And keep your voice down! Whatever's out there is going to hear you."

D-Rail took a small step toward me.

Steve growled, "Don't make me fuck you up, Hesston, you fucking traitor."

Shelly grabbed her boyfriend's arm. "Steve, he's right. Please calm down. There's something out there." Eyes wide, she craned her head and swept the darkened jungle floor.

Quickly Steve turned and raised his open palm toward her. Shelly grimaced and took a slow step back. "I've had enough from you," he growled.

"Come on, Steve," Les whined. "Quit freaking out."

Steve jabbed a finger toward his bassist. "Rest your neck, fat boy."

Defeated, Les dropped his head and stared at the ground.

I took a step toward Steve and stood my ground. "I've had enough of your shit. Just like you, we're all having a bad fucking day. I've already seen some pretty messed up shit, and the last thing any of us need is your loud ass mouth giving us away to whatever the hell is out there looking for us, or whatever doesn't even know we're here."

"What did you see?" Shelly asked.

My face shook, mouth tasting like batteries. "My dad."

"What?"

"I don't really want to talk about it."

The entire time Steve leered at me, waiting for me to make a move. The only move I made was a step backwards when I saw the red drain from his face.

"Your dad?" he finally asked.

I nodded. "I'd rather not discuss the details."

"Where did you see him?"

He was clearly not getting the point. "At the van."

"And where is he now? Does he have a car?"

"A phone?" Shelly asked.

"No!" I yelled. "He's not here! He and the van are gone!"

Les threw up his hands. "Woah, wait. Your dad took our van?"

"No, goddamn it! My Dad and the van disappeared."

"Disappeared?" Steve asked. "Like he drove off with it?"

I felt like punching them all, wondering what made me think finding them again was going to solve. "Look...they're gone. My dad. The van. Poof! Campbell's Soup. We now have to find another way out of this God forsaken place and we need to do it fast."

Steve eyed me. I couldn't tell if he meant to keep on about my dad or not, but he thankfully let it go. "OK then, Hesston. The van's gone, or so you say. It's all gone. Now what?"

"We keep searching for a phone or a way out of town, but since I highly doubt we're going to find a phone, we need to figure out—"

I didn't get to finish my thought. Shelly screamed and D-Rail pulled her backwards as Steve backed into me and we both fell over to the ground.

Thick branches wrapped around Les' waist and hair as the nearest tree hoisted him in the air. High above, Les squealed and squirmed as leafy branches and vines twirled around him, encasing his arms and legs in various shades of green. Down below, barky eyes blinked and glared at us as they held our bandmate tight.

"Fucking do something!" Les shrieked.

None of us could speak, could only gawk as the surrounding vines snaked their way up the tree's trunk and cocooned his limbs. Soon, his head was the only visible part of his body. A single vine crawled up his chest, and before Les could scream it pushed past his mouth and down his throat. Les gagged and went rigid. Tears rolled down his face. I pushed Steve off me, then stood and backed myself against the building front.

The surrounding trees turned to us and scowled, as if begging us to intervene. They reached up and added their own wooden arms to Les' canopy shell.

I knew what was coming next.

As they stared us down, they simultaneously pulled. His mouth full, Les was not able to scream as his body was yanked in every direction. Shelly and I screamed for him. Steve and D-Rail only watched in dismay.

With a loud pop, Les was separated into numerous pieces. Blood rained down, splashing the jungle floor and showering us all with his insides. I retched, but Steve was the first to evacuate his stomach. Somehow D-Rail had shielded Shelly from the gore, blanketing her while taking the brunt of the mess. Steve and I were not as lucky. Blood cascaded down my face, warm and pungent, and directly into my eyes. For a moment I could not see, and it scared me so badly I began to swing my arms to ward anything away. I did my best to blink away the red, and when I did the first thing I saw was Steve's bare back as it darted through the trees.

"Motherfucker!" I growled.

D-Rail, drenched like a Stephen King nightmare, grabbed Shelly by the wrist and ran for Steve. Shelly screamed hysterically, batting at his grip.

The massive tree that quartered Les glowered at

me, holding me in place. It slowly leaned in until it was only a few steps away. Its roots strained and groaned. It whispered, *"It's only going to get worse."*

Eyes clamped shut, I shook my head. "No, no, no!" I cringed as a branch full of leaves touched the side of my head. They rustled as they slid down my face, caressing me like a lover about to wish me goodnight. Les' cold fluids smeared my cheek and I could feel it on my lips as twig lightly pushed past my mouth. Earth and bark seized my taste buds. I couldn't move.

Another branch crept around the back of my neck and gently pushed my head forward. Knotted bark grazed against my teeth. I gagged as the leafy twig hit my tonsils and scraped the back of my throat.

Eyes shut, the tree moaned.

Vomit raced up my throat and before it reached the twig, I ripped it from my mouth. Two of my front teeth came flying out with it. Thick sap dripped from the twig's tip. The branch behind my head whipped forward, but I had already dropped to my knees to puke. The pain in my gums throbbed, but the sting from the twig slapping my cheek hurt much worse. The open gash sang as I rolled on the ground, avoiding another swipe as the tree aimed to hit me again. I reached up and snagged the branch and quickly snapped it in half.

From somewhere deep in the earth, the tree screamed. It thrashed its branches, leaves raining across the ground. I took my opportunity to run. I got to my feet and took off in the direction of the other three, weaving through the winding path of trees that scowled as I darted past. Branches and vines slapped at my face and arms, opening more skin to bleed freely. I could barely feel it. Though I had no idea where the others went, I pushed forward, adrenaline guiding me.

I focused on my breathing, counting my heartbeat in my empty gums.

As I reached the end of the block the earth beneath me rumbled and before I could dart across the street, two trees crossed in a massive X, blocking my path. I immediately cut left and sprinted down the path.

I quickly found myself entering yet another residential area, but only two houses sat staring at one another from across the street. At the end of the street the dark jungle seemed to call for me to disappear into its inky black. For a moment I nearly did just that. My brain told me to stop and slip into one of the houses, but my legs informed me the local plant life wanted to make me bleed.

The ground beneath me trembled. In the quake my foot found an unearthed root, and I tumbled to the ground. The ground cracked and split wide open. I sat up and crawled backwards, away from the growing pit.

From beneath the ground a massive hand lifted over the lip of the pit and dropped down in front of me. Each finger was its own tree, ancient gnarled bark popping and cracking as it dug into the dirt. Another hand followed, smashing the ground beside me.

"*Spence!*"

Shelly was leaning out the door of the house on my left, frantically waving me toward her. I wasted no time. I had no desire to see what was about to reveal itself from beneath the ground. The earth still shaking, I climbed to my feet and ran for the house.

Before I made it to the steps I caught another flash of white from the corner of the house.

Taking the steps two at a time, I pushed past Shelly and slammed the door shut as an unholy cry roared out behind me.

***

Shelly slammed the door shut and hugged me hard as I stumbled into the house. Fear momentarily stifled, I was immediately weary of being in another strange lodging. My eyes shot up to the ceiling, then back down to the floor. In the middle, I found Steve and D-Rail leering. Not relieved or happy. Leering.

Shelly whispered in my ear, "I'm so glad you're OK. Thought you were dead."

"Yeah, Hesston," Steve said, sternly, "we thought you were dead."

I quickly pushed Shelly off me and took a small step away. The blood running down my face and arms had grown cold and tacky, and despite the warmth it made me shiver. I spat a thick wad of red on the floor, and when I tasted the earthy wood once more, it made my stomach lurch. I dropped to a knee and vomited on the floor. Stomach acid burned the empty spaces in my gums. I started to cry, hard. I couldn't control it. My body shook like a wobbly tire. I had to place my hands flat in the squishy bile to keep from falling completely over. If I did fall I feared I might not get up again. Shelly knelt down beside me and pressed her face against my back and cried harder. I didn't bother to push her away. Although I loathed her, the warmth of her contact was, albeit the situation, comforting.

"Get up, you fucking crybabies."

I groaned, this time from anger.

"Say that again?"

"I said get up, you—"

I don't know what came over me. Even after everything that happened I still get grossed out thinking about it. I grabbed a handful of slimy puke and lobbed it at Steve. With a wet slap it hit him in the chin and sloshed against his bare chest. He froze, wide-eyed, unsure how to react. Behind him, D-Rail crinkled his nose in disgust. I knew he wanted to come after me, but he wanted no part of being covered in half digested pizza and ham sandwiches.

I stood and took a heavy step toward him. "How dare you!" I squeezed my fists, stomach fluids running down my hands. "A man just died—our bandmate just fucking died—or did you not see that? Obviously you did see it because you and Jason Voorhees behind you are covered in it."

Steve still hadn't moved, but his eyes narrowed as I took another step.

"Do you have no empathy, you bastard? Two of our bandmates are dead! Two of our friends are fucking dead! Two *human beings* were murdered by God-knows-what, and you have the balls to act like we're, what, selfish for mourning them? You pathetic excuse for a man."

Steve finally wiped the bile from his face and chest. "You want to join them?" He snapped his fingers, and behind him D-Rail dug into his back pocket and produced a small switchblade which he handed to Steve. He pointed it at me and released the blade. "Keep talking, Hesston."

Shelly placed her hand on my shoulder to pull me back. "Steve, put the knife away!"

I continued, tears rolling down my cheeks, "Do you have anything to say about Vinnie or Les? Anything in that whiskey-soaked peanut brain of yours?"

"Completely replaceable."

"Excuse me?"

"Do you have shit in your ears, Hesston? I said they're replaceable. I can find another drummer and bassist. They can learn the songs quick." He jabbed the knife at me, forcing me to take a step back. "You, on the other hand…I don't plan on finding another loud-mouth guitar player before next week."

"Have you ever considered there won't be a next week?" I screamed. Knife or not, I took another step toward him. D-Rail tensed and stepped closer to Steve. "And what makes you think I would want anything to do with you after all of this? We don't even know where we are. Every time we step outside, the landscape fucking changes! And even if we do somehow manage to get out of here, do you really think I would stick around and play with you? You're out of your fucking mind! The tour is dead—the band is dead!"

"*No, it's not!*" he screamed. "The tour remains on!"

"If it's not already obvious, Steve, I quit."

Steve bared his teeth. "You *what?*"

"I'm not repeating myself, you prick."

"You don't quit on me! Nobody quits on me!"

"*Please stop screaming!*"

The four of us froze. A fifth, unfamiliar voice yelled out from the back of the room. "You're being too loud."

"Hello?" Shelly asked.

"Shhhh…" the voice called back softly.

The location of the person shushing us was hard to pinpoint. The room we were occupying was a windowless, single doored living room, void of furniture.

Steve, searching for the voice, still had the blade pointed at me. D-Rail crept to the back corner and Shelly and I, giving Steve a wide berth, followed.

In the far back corner, about midway up the wall, we found a face.

Eyes closed, the man's face was almost as much a part of the wall as the flowery wallpaper surrounding it.

Had I not been looking for it I would have walked right past it. It was smooth like drywall, almost porcelain in shine. He looked asleep.

Steve reached out to poke it with his knife.

Its eyes suddenly snapped open, and Shelly screamed.

"Shhhh!" the face hissed. Then he whispered, "Please, for the love of God, stop making noise! You'll wake him!"

"Wake who?" I asked.

"Fuck that," Steve blurted, pointing the blade point at the wall. "Who are you, man? Where are we?"

The man's eyes shot back and forth like a Kit-Cat clock, not focusing on any of us. His breaths came in rapid rasps.

Steve jabbed the blade toward the man's face, close to his eyes. "I asked you a question, fucker. Who are you?"

"I...I-I-I don't know."

"Where are we?"

"No idea."

"Do you have a...body somewhere back there?"

The face seemed to consider this, eyes bouncing up and down. "Don't know."

I dropped down to a knee and got myself level with him. "Hey, man. What's your name? Let's start with that."

"I...can't remember."

"OK, well how long have you been here?"

Tears spilled down his glassy cheeks. "I...have no idea. It's been so long."

Part of me wanted to wipe his cheeks because he couldn't. "Listen, man. I want to help you—*we* want to help you—but we need you to help us, OK? Deal? We're just looking for a way out of this place."

The man's eyes closed. He sighed, "No way out."

Shelly knelt down with me. "What do you mean no way out?"

"Please stop talking. You're going to wake him."

"Wake who?" she asked.

Though he had no neck he shook his head. "Please don't wake him."

Steve had clearly had enough. "Listen, you fuck, you're going to tell us how to get out of here, or I'm going to cut your fucking eyeballs out and make you eat them. Got it?"

Eyes clamped shut, the man continued to shake his head.

"*I said got it?*"

The man opened his eyes and looked directly at Steve. He didn't say anything at first, only stared. "The man. In Milwaukee. You killed him."

Steve glared, fists clenched. "What?"

"After your show you killed him. I see everything. You took him outside after the show and you broke his neck. All because he touched—" his eyes turned to Shelly "—her."

Disgusted, Shelly pulled a face at her boyfriend. "What did you do, Steve?"

"Oh, you're no angel," said the face. "You've been sleeping with Spencer for months. Every chance you two are alone. Like rabbits."

Shelly and I stood up and slowly backed away. Teeth bared, Steve turned to us. His knuckles popped around the grip on the knife. "You did what?"

"Steve," Shelly cried, putting her hands up, "he's lying. I would never—"

"Never what, bitch?" he finished. "Fuck another man besides me?"

Shelly carefully sidestepped away from me, leaving

me by myself. "Steve, I swear I would never do that. I love you, baby!"

"*I love you, baby!*" he mocked. "I knew it. You're such a lying fucking bitch. I knew you were screwing around. I just had that feeling."

I put my hand up. "Woah, Steve, calm down. We can explain."

He screamed, "Explain what, motherfucker? That you've been fucking my girl behind my back? Who's the pathetic excuse now, Hesston?"

"That's not all he's done."

I turned back to the face on the wall. He was staring directly at me. "He was planning on quitting the band as soon as you went back home. He and Vinnie. Both were going to walk away. Just like that."

I grimaced, but the face made no expression. He only stared into my eyes, breaking my trust.

Somehow Steve managed to look angrier than he had only moments before. He pointed the knife at my face. "You're dead, Hesston! I'm going to slice you into fucking ribbons, you and that cheating whore."

Shelly cried, "Please, Steve!"

"*Shut up!*"

The face on the wall howled. "Stop screaming, you're going to wake—"

Before he could finish, D-Rail stepped toward it and punched him in the nose. A wet crunch followed. Wide eyed, the face appeared stunned, and for a moment it silenced him.

His eyes found mine. "Oh God, he's awake!" He then screamed, long and hard, forcing everyone to step away from the wall. As much as he could, he writhed and shook as if trying to free himself from his plaster prison. Blood dripped from his eyes, then down his nose, pattering the floor beneath. "Look what you've done!"

From each nostril, two small red hands slipped out and gripped each side. The wall-ridden face howled as the skin on his nose began to split and tear open like a clam. Blood sprayed, and I had to jump back to avoid its arc. With a wet pop, something small leapt from the man's face and hit the floor. Steve and D-Rail took a quick step back, and I put my arm across Shelly, urging her to do the same. The creature chittered and stood up to face us. Though it was small in stature, its arms and legs were long and lanky, with tiny horns that crowned its oblong skull. Little red eyes blinked as it scanned us over. The creature hissed—

—and before it could move, D-Rail's size fifteen came crashing down on it.

The creature went from upright to goo in a matter of seconds. Blood and bone slopped out from under his boot, and the creature's squeal was cut short. D-Rail turned to us and smiled dumbly.

The floor rumbled under our feet. At first I thought it was an earthquake, yet another thing in this plane of existence trying to off us, but D-Rail's stomping foot slowly rose in the air. A wave of tarantula sized spiders rose from the slop under heel, hundreds of them. Though their bodies appeared normal enough, their eight legs were made of human fingers, each one with long pointed nails that clicked the wooden floor as they skittered. Shelly and I quickly backed away toward the front door. Steve didn't move. He stood eerily still with the knife still clutched in his grip. The spiders swarmed up D-Rail's massive frame, fingers and fangs greeting exposed skin.

It was right about then I realized I had never heard D-Rail speak. Not a word or a mumble or grunt in my direction. Just dead, dumb eyes. Maybe he conversed with Steve when we weren't around, but I knew right then it was all for good reason. I had never heard a man with a voice that high scream in terror.

"*Get them off me! Get them off meeee!*"

Part of me wanted to help him, but those giant hands around my throat earlier reminded me he was on his own in this mess. More than anything I wanted to laugh.

"*Get them the fuck off me, Steve!*" He swiped at the softball sized arachnids, but they quickly crawled up his arms and pierced more skin. Steve finally stepped up and swiped the creatures with his switchblade, narrowly missing D-Rail's skin as he lobbed them across the room.

"Hold still, Goddamn it!"

D-Rail's skin immediately swelled around the bites, his skin turning fat and purple. He spun, around and around, bashing his arms and back against the wall. The spiders that didn't splat on the wall dropped to the floor and began to crawl our way. I didn't care to know what a bite from one of those awful things felt like, so I pulled Shelly toward the front door and ripped it open.

Outside, the amount of white was blinding. My foot missed the top step of the porch, and I fell face-first to the ground below. Behind me Shelly screamed. Fortunately the snowbank below broke my fall. I immediately sat up, the sudden extreme cold a jolt to my system. Beyond the yard, the jungle had become a whiteout so thick the house across the street was not visible. I almost wished the trees were back. There was something infinitely more terrifying barely being able to see beyond your nose.

Something white flickered in the street ahead.

I turned to reach for Shelly, but was greeted with cold steel as it sliced my face. My cheek opened up, and the following blood immediately froze as it poured. I tumbled backwards away from Steve as he swung again. He looked at me no longer as an ally or a bandmate. I was now the kid that broke his favorite toy. The boy who tripped him in front of the whole lunchroom. The guy who repeatedly fucked his girlfriend. Even over the icy wind I heard the growl crawling up his throat.

"Steve! Please stop! We can talk about this!"

The knife sliced through the air, inches from my face.

"I'm going…to…fucking…kill you…Hesston," he rasped. Snow and sleet pelted his bare chest.

I continued to back up slowly into the yard, several inches of snow fall building up around my bare ankles. Steve stayed with my every step. If he took a run at me, I had no idea if I could fight back. I simply didn't have the strength. I shot a quick glance toward Shelly, but the porch and house had already disappeared in plummeting white.

"Steve, please! I'm sorry!"

For a moment Steve looked as if he were going to cry. He cocked his head like a dog, considering my plea. "You're sorry? *You're sorry!* Sorry for what? Sorry for fucking my girlfriend? You know what, Hesston? I'm not all that surprised. I had an inkling it was happening. I wasn't sure though. I knew she liked you, but I always thought she knew better. I've done much worse things to guys for far less than this. I guess I was wrong about you. I was wrong about a lot of things." He lashed out quick. Before I could react, the blade sliced across the palm of my outstretched hand. "I was wrong about her." He swiped again, but missed. "Wrong about you." Missed again. "Wrong about everything!"

I held my hand and took another couple of steps until my back hit the waist high fence that bordered the property. "I'm so sorry, Steve. I never meant to hurt you."

"You're sorry you were caught! I gave you everything! I gave you a band, a tour, money—hell, and apparently I was giving you free pussy too!" He stopped walking and slumped his shoulders. "You were like a brother to me."

I laughed out loud. I couldn't help it. "A brother? Steve, I'm not sure how you haven't noticed but I've hated your guts since day one. Eat shit, you coward."

Steve visibly tensed. His fists shook. Then he growled and lunged forward—

—but Shelly leapt on his back, crossing her arms around his throat.

She screamed, "Put the knife down, Steve!"

"Get off me, you fucking bitch!" He spun in circles, but she kept her grip on him. She grabbed his frozen hair and yanked, then drew her fingernails across his forehead. Steve howled in pain, blood dripping into his eyes and freezing. He thrust his arm forward then back, catching Shelly in the stomach with his elbow. She gasped and fell from his back. Steve roared and spun, slashing his knife hand toward her.

I stopped breathing. Couldn't move. Steve also froze in place, realizing what he had done. He dropped the bloodstained knife.

Shelly gagged, unsteadily stumbling backwards in the foot high snow. Bright red blood drained from her throat, freezing as it reached her collarbone. Her eyes rolled back, as did her head, revealing a three inch deep cut that ran from ear to ear. The further her head lolled back, the more the skin ripped. Her legs finally gave out, and she collapsed to the ground.

Steve screamed and rushed to his girlfriend.

I wanted to join him, but something large materialized from the white behind them and bounded toward me. I had no time to react. D-Rail's hulking figure crashed into me and pinned me against the fence, his massive hands at my throat once again. He didn't hold back, squeezing as hard as his body would allow. And though it was quite a grip, I knew it wasn't his all. His arms and face, covered in massive spider bite welts, had already swollen to more than twice their normal size. Much like the excess poison dripping from the wounds, his pale skin had darkened to a deep shade of purple, as did his eyes and hair. To be frank, he looked like a wrong shade of Hulk.

"*I hate you! I hate you! I hate you!*" he cried in his falsetto voice.

I tried to fight back but I didn't have to do much. The toxin coursing through his veins continued to swell him, and his fingers loosened because of it. I twisted from his grip, gagging for air, and tossed myself to where Steve had dropped the knife. I frantically swept away snow and chunks of ice, but it sounded as though I wasn't going to need it.

Behind me, D-Rail fattened as his skin continued to bloat. He screamed long and hard, his voice reaching octaves I didn't think were humanly possible. I gave up on the knife and took a step back from him, and another, and another. By the time I found the opening of the fence to the street, D-Rail resembled a McDonald's Grimace.

Violet, you're turning violet!

D-rail shot me one last painful look, spittle bubbling around his mouth—

—then he popped.

Much like Les, bright purple gore showered over

me. For a moment I almost relished the splash of warmth, but the reek drew me out of it. I gagged and heaved, but I had nothing left in me. When I wiped my eyes I found almost nothing left of D-Rail but a ten foot circle of frozen lavender. On the other side stood Steve.

"What did you do?" he asked.

"What did *I* do? *What did I do?* He fucking exploded, you moron!"

Steve dropped to his knees and hung his head. "I have nothing left."

"*You've still got me, baby...*"

Steve shot up so fast it made me jump. Behind him, something rose from the snow. He backed up over the leftover D-Rail which crunched under his feet.

Shelly sat up awkwardly and rose to her feet, her head and arms lolling about like a marionette puppet. Eyes closed, her head finally settled backwards and it opened up her knife gash wider. Rows of razor sharp teeth lined the wound, creating a new mouth that seemed to grin at us.

"Sh...Shelly?" he whispered.

"I'll always be by your side, Steve. You too, Spence. I love you both so very much." A long forked black tongue rose from her throat and ran across her teeth. She clutched her breasts. "Mmmm, I'm so wet. I want you both right now! Right here in the snow!"

Steve continued to back away, and I felt my frozen feet do the same.

"Awww, where you going, boys? The fun's just getting started!"

Arms cradling his chest, Steve shivered and quaked. The cold finally appeared to be working on him.

"You're dead..." he whispered.

She rasped, "*You're next*," then ran straight at us.

Steve screamed, then turned and ran toward me. He shouldered past me, then took a left and bounded down the street. In a few moments he was gone in the blizzard. I broke my daze and ran in the opposite direction, though I wasn't sure which one us of was being followed. When I heard slushy uneven footsteps behind me, it became clear.

"Spencer, baby, come back to me!"

I pushed hard, completely unaware of what direction I was going. My feet left the sidewalk and the ground beneath me became increasingly impassable. The further into town I got, the higher the snow drifts became. My feet and legs were numb, and my arms pumping were the only thing keeping them warm.

"I want you so bad, baby!" she called out from somewhere close behind. *"Don't you remember Vegas?"*

I found a small space between two buildings and squeezed myself in. Yes, I did remember Vegas. Pretty well, in fact. But I had no desire to recreate that night with anything that owned teeth like that. I kept quiet and waited for her to pass.

Nothing surprised me anymore. I wasn't shocked by this, or even angry. I just wanted to go home. I waited there, shivering against cold brick until it seemed as if the coast was clear. I did not hear her unsteady feet kicking through the snow, or her raspy breaths bubbling from the hole in her neck. After what seemed like hours the snowfall had finally stopped, leaving only a light breeze behind in its wake. I leaned my head against the wall and closed my eyes. Then I heard it—

A low rumbling under my feet. I pressed my ear against the wall and listened to the purr as it steadily ramped up. I knew that sound. I carefully shuffled out from my hiding spot and into what appeared to be the town's center. The immediate street ahead circled a large statue of a man, though I wasn't sure who it was supposed to be. The surrounding buildings were dark and quiet, the snow blanketing them glistening in the sun. I stepped closer to the street's edge and waited as the motorcycles approached.

My heart fluttered as a pack of bikers roared around the corner and into the town square, eight of them all together. Though I had learned quickly to not trust a single thing in this terrible place, not even my own eyes or gut, I nearly cried at the sight of fellow humans that didn't belong to my own party. I took another hopeful step out onto the sidewalk and waited for them to round the statue before they came to a halt at the curb in front of me. They lined up and switched their motors off. I wanted to cry for joy.

Leather pants and jackets creaking, they approached me, each one towering over me by an extra foot, faces shielded by helmets. For a moment they stood there, watching me. I didn't know what to say. I was waiting for the other shoe to drop, waiting for that hopeful fluttering of my stomach to seize itself back into a ball of misery.

"I..."

One by one they removed their gloves and helmets, and I knew right then I would never leave this place.

The closest one stepped forward and stood over me, looking me up and down with his thin, vertical pupils. Two long pointed incisors poked out from the corners of his mouth, and his hairy cheeks fluffed out in two wispy points that vibrated as he purred. Two pointed ears twitched as they waited for my response. I had none.

He was a fucking cat.

Behind him, the other man-animals regarded me with little interest. They poked and prodded one another, shaking off their riding stiffness. Behind the cat, three dogs laughed and pointed at me: a Pitbull with deep scars zigzagging over his cheeks and forehead, a beady-eyed Chihuahua, and a Boxer with saggy cheeks and an upturned nose. The other four were cats of various shades and colors, longhairs and tabbies, oranges, blacks and browns. The cat-man before me was almost beautiful had he not been terrifying. Soft gray hair covered this angular face, with a creamy white shading his muzzle and ending at a point between his green eyes. He looked exactly like my cat Ozzy. So much, in fact, that I nearly reached up to pet him.

"We heard there's a concert here tonight." His voice was deep and dripping in New York sass.

I couldn't speak, could only focus on the cat's long whiskers as he stared me down.

"Yo, I'm talkin' to you, shrimp." He nudged me with his paw. "Where's the fuckin' concert?"

"Concert?" I croaked.

The Pitbull stepped up and nudged me too, his paw raking my chest. "Listen up, fucknuts. We just rode a very long way to see a concert. It wouldn't be very wise to cancel on us, I can tell you that!"

"I-I-I don't know what you're talking about..."

"You're Spencer Hesston, right?" the cat asked. "Of Rot in Hell? We heard about yous going solo and all, and we came an awful long way to see you play."

I didn't realize it until I lifted my foot but I had already backed away two steps, and the cat noticed before I did. He grabbed me by my shirt collar and pulled me in close. The stink of animal breath wafted in my face.

"Listen, kid. We haven't gotten our twelve to

sixteen hours of sleep today. I believe it would be in your best interest to just get on that stage and rock the fuck out." He threw a hairy thumb over his shoulder.

I looked over him and found a stage set up against the large statue in the square, with eight folding chairs set up in front. In the middle of the stage was my missing guitar and amplifier and nothing else. I turned back to the cat who gave me an 'Understand?' look. I hesitantly nodded, and he dropped me. I rubbed the claw indents on my chest.

Through the snow, the cat ushered me to the stage and waited for me to walk up the side steps before the rest took their seats. I approached my Les Paul, and part of me was thrilled to finally see it again. I didn't realize how much I actually missed it until I picked it up and slung it over my shoulder. It felt good around my neck, normal and real. The guitar was already plugged in, and the amp already warming up. I clicked on the bypass and I stiffened. I suddenly had no idea what to do. I had never been on a stage by myself. I was usually surrounded by chaos, drums and bass in sync, a large shirtless man roaring about death and destruction. On stage I enjoyed having eyes on me, watching my hands and my timing, but I was never the main focus. This was very foreign to me. I turned and eyed the animals who had come to watch me play.

"Play something!" the Boxer called out.

One of the cats, a flat-faced Persian, laughed, "Yeah, don't be a pussy!"

I shivered. The cold had numbed my bare limbs, and I couldn't feel my hands across the strings. I slowly rolled the volume up on my guitar, and the amp behind me hummed to life. Steeling myself, I closed my eyes, grabbed the pick from the headstock, then took a deep breath and played...

My fingers began to tingle as Van Halen's "Eruption" exploded over the fretboard. The distortion was sudden and frantic, my fingers rushing along the strings with a fine tuned memory. I didn't have to think about it. My brain flushed to my hands and they did all the work for me. I shut myself down and let the music carry me away. My pick trilled the unwound strings, and somewhere deep in my subconscious I hoped I was making Wolfgang's daddy proud. Then Van Halen became Led Zeppelin, the solid groove of "Heartbreaker" making my knees and legs sway, which naturally bled into "Living Loving Maid". My hands gripped the neck tighter as groove became gallop with Metallica's "One", the song's rapid fire bridge pounding the stage beneath my feet. Song after song, melody after melody, lick after lick, effortlessly poured from my soul. I couldn't stand still. The air around me crackled. I jumped from side to side. I headbanged. I thrashed. As AC/DC appeared, I shuffled and danced like Angus Young. I didn't give a fuck. I didn't care who was watching. I played with every fiber of my being, and the world around me responded. A dull whisper became a loud roar as the air around me heated, and sweat dripped steadily down my face in response. Suddenly I was indoors, surrounded by thousands of filled seats, the floor writhing like maggots, every soul chanting in unison HESS-TON HESS-TON HESS-TON, and I obliged them. I soaked up their energy, used to speed my hands, my mind. I D-tuned on the fly and ripped through Lamb of God and In Flames, Nirvana and Rage Against the Machine, Foo Fighters and Mötley Crüe. I didn't care what I played. The audience didn't care. They cried and shouted in jubilation, thrilled to be there, to see me, to witness my all. The volume rose, lactic acid burned, fingers cramped. I dropped to my knees at the edge of the stage, my head thrown back, mouth screaming, and my B and high E strings finally gave out and snapped in unison. The crowd suddenly went quiet, and all that was left was me. I pulled one last pinch-harmonic from my strings and let the note ring out before finally rolling down the volume. Ears ringing, heart racing, I slowly opened my eyes...

...and nothing had changed. I was still there, surrounded by snow and the eyes of animal bikers. Sweat froze on my hair and face, and my arms shivered against the lacquered wood of my guitar. In the distance, a white blur shifted between two buildings but disappeared after I blinked. I instead focused on the crowd of eight before me.

They were quiet, some leaning over, hands in laps, while others sat back with arms folded across their chests. I couldn't read them. They looked bored, like I had forced them to sit through a college lecture and I was now asking for questions. I didn't know what to say.

The gray and white cat eventually sat up, then stood. Paws cupped around his mouth, he yelled, "Boooo!" The rest of them stood and joined him with their own jeers.

I sighed and sunk into myself, nearly collapsing on my side.

I was done.

Something heavy exploded in a wet mush on the stage next to me, followed by two more. By the time I realized what they were I was struck in the face. Tomato juice dripped down my face, stinging my eyes. I tried to stand but ripe red fruit rained down on me like a storm. I covered my head, and they continued to pelt my every exposed part. The bikers howled with laughter, savoring my pain, as they tossed their armfuls.

I pounded the stage with my fist, once, twice, and then slowly pushed myself up on my knuckles. I took a deep breath, gathering my will to face them. I didn't care anymore. I wouldn't cry. I wouldn't give up. I wouldn't let this place break me any longer. They had not killed me yet, and I wasn't going to stand by and let weather, creatures, or flying fruit put me under. I rose to face the bikers and, with everything I had, I screamed. The cats and dogs immediately stopped their throwing and watched me curiously, ears perked, their heads cocked to the side. I belted out my soul, fists tight and clamped at my sides. I roared until my breath failed me. When I finished I pulled my Les Paul over my shoulder and, still plugged in, lobbed it at the cat up front. Behind me, the cable snapped tight and sent my amp head crashing to the stage.

The gray and white cat ducked as my guitar sailed over his head and came crashing into a row of folding chairs behind him. He turned, wide-eyed, and hissed, baring his claws. The other cats, too, were startled, their hair fluffing up in defense. The dogs crouched low and barked, their lips frothing with white foam.

I ran. I had no other choice. My heart wanted me to plant myself on that stage and let them come at me. I wanted to fight, I wanted to hit something and feel it break beneath my fists. I was tired of hiding, tired of seeing people die, tired of that feeling of lost hope every time I stepped outside, but my brain told me to beat feet. I did the smart thing and trusted my instincts. I leapt off the side of the stage and took off toward the entrance of town. Behind me, the dogs howled and bounded through the snow after me.

Though I had no desire to hide any longer, I didn't know where to go. Every house or building I stepped foot in brought its own horrors, never mind the ones outside. I had to keep running, leave this Godforsaken town, and see what was beyond the border. I could no longer feel my lower body, my feet and legs completely numb as I rushed through the ankle high snow. My arms tingled as I pumped them to keep ahead of my pursuers. Barks and yips joined numerous feet as they loped after me. They weren't men anymore. They didn't even stand upright. They bounded on all fours, gnashing their teeth and jowls at my backside as they gradually caught up. I pushed harder, staying just a few extra steps ahead.

I came around the corner and found myself back on the first street we had entered town from. Ahead of me, the road that lead out of town was a white blur, the landscape beyond so bright it was hard to focus on. It was where I wanted to be, where I had to be, and the town itself realized that. The still air became heavy with moisture, and snow and sleet fell over me in a sudden wave. Ice pellets shelled me, and I had to shield my eyes from the attack. I didn't care. At that point the forces that be could have dropped a house on my head, and I would have found a way through it. Building after building rushed past. I kept low, and ran headfirst into the storm...but another force of nature came crashing into me.

Though my face was numb, I felt every knuckle of Steve's fist as it caved into my cheek. I never saw him coming. I left my feet and fell sideways to the ground. My head buried, Steve reached into the snow and seized my hair and pulled. I couldn't resist. I swam in and out of unconsciousness, and the last thing I saw before I passed out were the words SHOE REPAIR SHOP.

***

It wasn't a whisper or even a cold splash of water that woke me from my sleep—those would have been preferable. Instead, I woke to my nose being crushed and dented to the side of my head. Fists swung to and fro, battering my oblivious face. I coughed myself awake and immediately tried to fight him off with what little strength I still had. He was straddling me on a cold wooden floor, his weight keeping me from doing much other than pathetically flail my arms. Much like the other houses, the shoe repair shop was entirely bare, save for a doorway leading into a dark backroom. For some reason, I was a little disappointed there were no actual shoes.

"Wakey, wakey, Hesston! Time. For. Breakfast!" Steve accented every word with a strike.

My teeth rattled and loosened, and those jagged spaces where teeth once were ripped into my lips and tongue. His fist struck my forehead, and warm blood dripped down both sides of my head like a crown. My brain swam in a wave of nausea, and I knew I was concussed. I let my arms fall limp to the floor.

"What?" Steve huffed, out of breath. "You had enough, Hesston? Is it too much for you? Well guess what? *I haven't had enough!*" He grabbed cheeks and pinched my mouth. He leaned in close enough for his breath to warm my lips. "No matter what I do to you, you weaselly fuck, it'll never be enough to satisfy me."

I moaned and tried to speak, but he pinched harder. "I'm speaking! You don't get to say anything anymore, you hear me? In fact, I'm not sure you can say much anymore." He reached into my mouth and yanked out a loose incisor from my gums and let it clatter onto the floor. "At least not without a lisp."

Eyes closed, I let the waves of pain rock me into submission. My nerves pulsed to a beat of song I swore I knew, but I could not find the lyrics. I fought to find anything that made me happy: a heavy guitar riff, the face of an ex-girlfriend, my mom and dad. But I struggled to imagine anything that didn't have teeth ready to bite. I wanted freedom and a warm bed, and in that moment I prayed Steve would mercifully grant me one of those.

He stood and walked over to the window to peak out. "You know, I've come to the realization that we're probably not getting out of here. And that's OK. It took me a bit, but I think I've come to accept it. It sucks, though, I'm not going to lie. No more band. No more tours. I'm really going to miss shit on the outside, like beer and tacos. And pussy too, I guess."

For a brief moment I managed to open my swollen eyes. Steve craned his head, looking out the frosted window in both directions. I focused on his bare back. The duck with the dick was gone.

"You never cared, did you?" Steve turned away from the window with tears falling down his face. "About any of it."

"What?" I tried to sit up but immediately collapsed.

"All you wanted was to fuck my girlfriend and ruin my band, my life's work. You killed everything I ever loved, you miserable fuck." His eyes widened. He pointed at me, hand shaking. "You're from here, aren't you? You were sent to destroy me!"

Even though my eyes were quickly swelling shut, I still managed to roll them. "You're an idiot."

"And you're a monster! I knew it! You were sent to ruin me. You took my girlfriend from me, my best friend D-Rail, and my band. You're the fucking devil... and this is Hell. It all makes sense now. How did I not see it before?"

Air whistled through my broken nose. "We all woke up here. I'm not from here, you psycho. I'm not—fuck it. I'm done arguing with you."

Slowly, Steve approached me. He seemed frightened of me now, like he didn't want to get too close. "What did I do to deserve you?"

I sighed, "I ask myself the same thing."

"If only I still had my knife, I'd cut you open and see what's underneath."

On the far wall, a small wooden slat rustled and slid sideways revealing an empty black space. From inside, something small was tossed out onto the floor.

A pocket knife.

Steve carefully plucked up the knife and studied it. I watched his reaction with little surprise. He grinned and stepped toward me. Whatever he planned to do, I knew I couldn't stop him.

"You know...a knife just seems too quick. I want something a little more...blunt. A little gnarlier."

As if answering back, a small space in the ceiling directly above me broke open, and a large metal mallet fell from it and clattered to the floor. I winced as it dropped a few inches from my head.

"Much better!" Steve tossed the knife aside and straddled me once more. He grabbed the hammer, whose head was nearly five inches wide, and gripped the handle with white knuckles. "So... What shall we do first, hmmm?"

I couldn't move. My chest ached, and eyes were nearly swollen shut. I put my right palm against his chest.

With his free hand, Steve grabbed my wrist and squeezed. "Well, what do we have here? Oh, I know! You certainly can't play guitar with only one hand, correct? Which is this, your pick hand?" He repositioned himself, pressing his knee against my throat and my right arm against the floor. "It would certainly ruin your career if you couldn't play guitar anymore. I mean—a one-handed guitarist? Who's heard of such a thing?"

I gagged, his knee pressing hard against my wind pipe. "Steve! Please!"

Steve gritted his teeth, lifting the mallet higher. "Hesston, just shut up and take it."

With a solid *thump*, the bones in my index and middle fingers crunched and flatted as the mallet met my hand. At first I felt nothing, only a quick swell of pressure. It's when the mallet lifted off my skin I was finally greeted with pain. I screamed, my eyes rolling in their sockets. Suddenly my body was wide awake, adrenaline surging. My brain was fully alert, no longer swimming in the sea. I bucked underneath Steve, kicking and thrashing. He pushed his knee harder into my throat, stifling my agony.

"Hey, hey, hey, settle down. You're going to make me slip and break something." He guffawed and swung the mallet once more, this time finding my thumb and most of my palm. The pain blossomed and spread down my arm. Over my shrieking, I heard a wet squelch as he lifted the mallet. He shook it, letting my warm blood sprinkle across my face.

With all my body could muster, I howled as the mallet came crashing down, over and over. I kept wondering if at some point I wouldn't feel it any longer, that the agony would suddenly dissipate, and my brain would finally do me solid and let me pass out or die. But I remained wide awake for every thump the mallet made on the floor. At some point Steve started screaming along with me, mocking my stifled cries as he took away the only thing that made me *me*. Over and over, that mallet undid me. Took away my identity. Music faded from my ears. I was never going to buy my dad that new house he wanted.

At some point I stopped screaming, and the wet squishing noises the mallet had made stopped too. Above me, Steve huffed as sweat dripped down his face and chest.

He laughed, "Holy fucking hell, that was amazing! What a rush!" He sat back, exhausted, and took his knee off my throat. I gagged for air. "Goddamn, Hesston, that was the most fun I've had in a long time. Fuck, I think I might have cum in my pants."

I kept my eyes clamped shut, not daring to look at the ruin of my right hand.

Steve sighed and eyed the bloody mallet. "So, what's next? Your other hand? You can't play guitar with only one hand, but missing two? *No bueno, amigo.* What about your feet? Yeah! We can hobble you, like that bitch from the movie, where she had that writer dude strapped to a bed. That might be fun! Or maybe we can smash that cock of yours into mush, the one you used to fuck my girlfriend with?" He rubbed the hilt of the mallet against my crotch, then pressed down. "What do you think, Hesston? Should I let you decide, or should I just close my eyes and let the mallet decide? What's that, Mr. Mallet? We should break his face? I don't know, Mr. Mallet, won't that be too painful? You know what? You're right. You're absolutely right. He and that ugly ass mug of his *do* deserve it." He lifted the blood soaked mallet over his head and grinned. "He deserves all of it."

My hand obliterated, I no longer wanted to live.

I closed my eyes and waited to die.

BOOM!

The entire building shook, the wooden floor beneath

me creaking. My body quaked, and I wondered if his mallet had caused the racket.

BOOM!

"What the fuck is that?" Steve asked.

BOOM!

At first I thought it was an earthquake, and at the moment it wouldn't have surprised me in the least if it was, but the time between each tremor was a steady number you could count between.

They were footsteps.

Steve stood and stepped over me. I sucked in a deep breath and coughed up blood in response. When I turned my head I unwillingly caught sight of my hand. It caused me to throw up more. Skin and bones had been flattened and reshaped into a pink blob that was now more part of the floor than part of me. Only thin strands of skin were still attached to my wrist, keeping me somewhat grounded to the wooden planks beneath me. Blood steadily squirted from the wound. Without even thinking, I instinctively rolled over on my chest, ripping the rest of my hand skin from the floor. I shuddered, my body heat draining quick.

Mallet in hand, Steve slowly approached the doorway into the back room, and the heavy footsteps got louder and closer. He suddenly stopped and began to back up.

In the shadows, a massive white shape materialized and slowly stomped into the main room, one heavy step at a time. I blinked, my eyes clouding over, blurring the figure. When they cleared, I finally realized what had been stalking me since we arrived. I carefully sat up and scooted away toward the front door.

Steve stopped and dropped the mallet to the floor. He reached behind his back and rubbed the bare spot where his tattoo used to be.

He was almost cartoonishly large. Muscles flexed and rippled underneath layers of bright white feathers, his massive torso dwarfing the much smaller man before him. Much like the tattoo, the duck's giant hands were placed on his hips, and he thrusted his enormous human-like erection out with pride. His penis, as long as the duck was tall, throbbed, its demanding weight bouncing with each step of his webbed feet. The duck glared down at Steve, his bright orange bill somehow torqued into a scowl.

Steve dropped his hands, clearly in awe. "Wow... You look much better in person."

The duck snorted and leaned in until he was nearly touching Steve's face. In a deep, booming voice he said, "*QUACK.*" He leaned back, then grabbed the head of his penis and lifted it high over Steve's head. Steve screamed and before he could throw his hands up, the duck let go, and the massive organ slammed down onto the top of his head. Only a stifled grunt, and Steve's body folded up like an accordion. Blood exploded across the room, a wave washing over me and across the floor. I couldn't scream. I had to conserve the last of my energy.

The fowl tore his penis away from the mess on the floor, and it now seemed to point right at me. The duck cocked its head. "*QUACK?*"

With my only good hand I pointed at him, "No!" and quickly stood and went for the front door.

Ruined arm held against my chest, I threw the door open and stepped outside. Overhead, the sun was so bright I could barely see. I winced and leapt off the porch, and my feet immediately hit ankle deep water. The ground had become a soupy black pool, and though I wasn't sure of how deep the rest of the water was, I had to keep moving. With every bit of strength I had I ran toward the end of the street and past the edge of town.

I pushed hard, my breath coming in short bursts. Along with my empty gums my arm throbbed dully, and blood continued to drain steadily from my wrist, dropping into the water with my splashing feet. Though the water continued at the same level, my feet struggled to push through, and eventually I felt myself slowing. Vertigo hit me, and I swayed.

Behind me, a motorcycle revved, then several more roared to life. Dogs howled, and a few loud meows followed. My heart leapt, and I forced my legs to do the same. I pushed forth through the muck with no idea of where I was going.

Then it appeared. About fifty feet ahead, a large black circle blinked open at eye level. At that moment I didn't care what it was or where it lead to, I knew I had to be there. It was big enough for me to run straight into, and that's what I aimed for.

A large splash behind me begged for my attention. I didn't have to look. The giant dicked duck quacked and swam for me, his massive arms propelling him forward. Others joined him. Vines erupted from the water, slapping at me, almost playfully. The bikers drove through the muck, honking the horns as they approached. Vinnie and Shelly's voices called out as they attempted to catch up. Vinnie had become one of the sickly creatures that killed him, and Shelly's head lifelessly bobbed as her neck teeth snapped at the air. "Come back, Spencer!" she yelled. "Don't leave! Stay here with me! We can be together forever!"

"We can start our own band here, Spencer!" Vinnie rasped. "Steve will never bother us!"

I screamed and pushed hard for the hole.

The hole suddenly shrank, now half the size it was before. I ran harder.

To my left, two shark fins erupted from the water and headed right for me. To my right, tree limbs broke the water surface and grasped at my legs. Overhead, the sun, with a mouth and two eyes, smiled cheerfully and winked as I passed underneath.

Twenty feet from the hole, it grew smaller. I half expected a cartoon pig to pop out from the other side and exclaim "That's All Folks!"

Ten feet, and I felt Shelly's icy hands caress my shoulders. She whispered, "Don't leave me. I haven't tasted you yet," and hooked her clammy fingers into my mouth.

Five feet, and I leapt into the hole and tumbled face-first into oblivion.

***

And that's it. That's everything that happened. As ridiculous as it all sounded, I'll defend everything I wrote here until my dying breath, no matter what the police or the doctors say. They don't know. They weren't there. I've got the scars and the unserviceable stump to prove it.

They found me on the side of Interstate 69, not three miles from the edge of Evansville. Some passerby saw me on the shoulder and called the police. I was nearly dead from blood loss. They thought I had been in a wreck. Our van was found just a few miles back, flipped on its side in a ditch. There was nobody else there, and our belongings were missing.

That was almost seven months ago. It feels like much longer. Everything still hurts and I'm so tired much the time, and it doesn't help that I'm stuck in this fucking bed most of the day. The police won't let me leave. They questioned me for weeks, wanted to know where my bandmates were and why I was covered head to toe in their DNA. I told them everything, though I'm not surprised they didn't believe a single word of it. I guess I wouldn't either if I were them. After I went to the hospital, I was transferred to the Indiana State Hospital, where I've been ever since and will remain until 'more evidence is gathered.' They think I killed them. They can't find their bodies, and their parents think I did it. For the longest time I hated the way they looked at me, disgusted and accusing. Now I just don't care. The only thing I care about is my parents, and I haven't heard from either of them since I came back home. Not a word or a visit. The police told me they couldn't locate either of them. Both have turned up missing. I'm sure they think I did that too.

I hate it here. It's cold, the food sucks, and the caretakers and doctors treat me like some deranged criminal. I do what I can to get through the day. I don't have a TV or access to a computer, but I have caught up on my reading. I ache for my guitar. Sometimes I sit up at night and try to write riffs in my head, but for some reason I can't remember what a guitar even sounds like. It's the weirdest thing.

I have difficulty sleeping. At night I see things, terrible things. I don't think all of me made it out of that place. Sometimes I see a white blur. Other times I wake and I swear I see large spiders with human finger legs crawling down the ceiling and over my bed. I can still feel blood on my skin and taste it on my tongue.

They don't grant me much here, but they were gracious enough to give me this spiral notebook to write my feelings out on, which you hold here in your hands. I guess they're hoping at some point I would write out a confession or an apology or something. The only apology I can offer is for writing this entire thing out in crayons. As you can imagine, they won't allow me to use a pen or pencil or anything sharp, so a sixty-four color box of Crayola's was all I had to work with. Also writing left-handed when you're naturally a righty is about as awful as you'd think.

I don't know if anyone, the doctors or police or whoever, will read this. I don't really care either. They seem to have made up their minds about me, so why bother? Maybe this was just for me. Maybe I'll use these last few pages to write a song...if I can remember how. I've got the time. I don't think I'm going anywhere for a while.

The night nurse just came in and announced it was bath time. That's fine. I need a break. I'm tired of writing. Yes, a bath sounds really good right now.

I feel dirty.

Wesley Southard is the author of the novel *The Betrayed*, the novellas *Closing Costs* and *One For The Road*, and has had short stories appear in numerous outlets such as *Cover of Darkness Magazine*, *Eulogies II: Tales from the Cellar*, *Grindhouse*, *Dark Bits*, *Blood Reign Lit Magazine*, *The Book of Blasphemous Words*, and *Clickers Forever: A Tribute to J.F. Gonzalez*. When not watching numerous hours of ice hockey, he spends his free time reading and drinking copious amounts of green soda. He is also a graduate of the Atlanta Institute of Music, and he currently lives in South Central Pennsylvania with his wife and their cavalcade of animals. Visit him online at www.wesleysouthard. wordpress.com.